We Who Live Apart

Stories by

⤳ JOAN CONNOR ⤳

UNIVERSITY OF MISSOURI PRESS
COLUMBIA AND LONDON

Copyright © 2000 by Joan Connor
University of Missouri Press, Columbia, Missouri 65201
Printed and bound in the United States of America
All rights reserved
5 4 3 2 1   04 03 02 01 00

Library of Congress Cataloging-in-Publication Data

Connor, Joan.
    We who live apart : stories / by Joan Connor.
        p. cm.
    ISBN 0-8262-1293-X (alk. paper)
        I. Title.

PS3553.O514255 W4 2000
813'.54—dc21   00-041794

⊗™ This paper meets the requirements of the
American National Standard for Permanence of Paper
for Printed Library Materials, Z39.48, 1984.

Design and composition: Vickie Kersey DuBois
Printer and binder: Edwards Brothers, Inc.
Typefaces: Carolina, Gill Sans, Minion

This book is for my son,
Kerry Wessell,
who shows me the way home.

ᔆ Contents ᔆ

Acknowledgments

The following stories have been previously published, and some appeared in slightly different versions:

"We Who Live Apart," *Puckerbrush Review*

"October," *Mississippi Valley Review*

"The Thief of Flowers," *Antietam Review*

"Summer Girls," *Portland Monthly*

"And I, Isolde," *Arts & Letters*

"Women's Problems," *Slipstream*

"The Bowlville Cemetery," *BlueLine*

The author wishes to thank Lisa Ruffolo for her help in editing individual stories in the collection. She also wishes to acknowledge Marina Warner's *From the Beast to the Blonde*, for pointing out the mathematical conundrum at the heart of the Bluebeard tale, and Joseph Campbell's *Transformations of Myth through Time*, for its analysis of the Tristan and Isolde tale.

We Who Live Apart

The Thief of Flowers

Hadley Falls, "the flats" where the sooty, brick, Irish tenements squat by the river, where, in winter, the snow always seems dirtier than up on High Street where the mansions condescend to glance down the hill, where my grandmother keeps the apartment too warm and squirrels away dollars under the carpet's cabbage roses, under the yellow oilcloth on the table, or behind the paint-by-number seascape, the apartment where my dad's lived since my mother died of stomach cancer, where he curses the dim rooms that smell of boiled dinners and overwaxed furniture, and musty drapes, where fussy glass vases—a Santa boot, a green swan, a woeful-eyed cocker spaniel with a hole in the top of his head—beg for flowers but receive only dust, where my grandmother sits, smelling of the shot rubber in her girdle and the chemicals in her blued hair, where my brother, Danny, and I live like guests, sleeping in twin beds in my dead grandfather's bedroom, his cardigans dangling still in the closet, exhaling pipe tobacco, whiskey spittle, age, and illness, where we wait for my father to deliver on his promise to get us out of here, to someplace better, a ranch house in South Hadley, a bungalow on the River Road, anywhere but here. But there's no money since he lost his job at the paper mill, and Danny and I are terrified by this woman whose blue cotton-candy head is so low she's almost humped when she comes into our room at night and closes the window we've opened and who shoves cotton balls in our ears soaked with some oily medicine that smells like our mother's hospital death. And Grandma pulls all the venetian blinds so no light enters until she leaves and

1

Danny scrambles up and yanks the cord. We live together in a zebra-striped world of moonlight and night, holding our breaths, afraid of Grandma's smell and singsong voice, the sacred heart on her dresser and the rosary she mumbles to and the ashes of Mrs. Murphy in the dark dining room sideboard, who's damned to hell for cremating herself against the Church's express wishes, but Grandma, loving the Church and Mrs. Murphy, who lived above-stairs for thirty years, can't decide whether to scatter her or not, so, whenever we cross through the dining room, we tiptoe fast to get to the only bright room in the house—the kitchen, with its white porcelain sink and white gas appliances, its white walls and high ceiling and white wraparound porch where Grandma hangs her laundry that, this time of year, stiffens, starched with ice on the frozen cord until she, capitulating, gathers it and warms it dry in the low oven.

This morning I've been awake for hours and have removed the nasty cotton balls and tiptoed through the dining room and tossed them down the dumbwaiter shaft no one uses, and I've pulled my coat on over my clown pajamas that are as short in the sleeves and legs as my memory of my mother who gave them to me two Christmases ago. Sometimes at night I still hear her laugh, that laugh when she first saw the pom-pom buttons on my chest, bob-bing on Christmas Eve. The pom-poms fell off a year ago, and one by one I plucked the red yarns from the globe until nothing but a knot of thread was left.

I sneak out the kitchen door, but I'm back in the flat by 5:00 A.M. when Grandma rises by habit as if she were going to walk to morn-ing mass, but since we moved in, she watches the service in black and white on the Zenith and complains how she misses color, espe-cially the brilliant purple vestments of Easter. I don't think of Grandma as caring about color. But my mother loved color; her favorite was red. And she insisted on the TV. A modern novelty, she called it when we still lived in the ranch house. We're the only peo-ple in the neighborhood with a TV. Mom wanted a Hi-Fi next, then a spin washer. But she died before she got them.

Grandma's cooking lumpy oatmeal and murmuring to the rosary in the kangaroo pocket of her flowered apron, stirring with one hand, fingering the beads with the other. Danny skids into the kitchen and sits at the table with me, both of us dreading the beige clotted cereal. Then Dad bumbles in looking as unstrung as the swinging sash of his bathrobe. I'm fingering the contours of wadded dollars that Grandma tucks under the oilcloth when Danny startles me, hip-hops up from his chair, shrieking, "Snow! It snowed last night—it's still white!" And without asking permission, he's pulling on his red rubber boots over his PJ's and flapping out to the vestibule where the vases collect dust, and, bam, we can tell by the single slam that he's forgotten again to close the outer door.

I wait. Danny springs back in, dusted with sprinkly snow rainbows, smelling clean and cold and screaming, "A miracle. Flowers are blooming in the snow, roses and some red stuff, too."

"Carnations," I say.

And Danny cocks his head at me. "How do you know?"

I look down at the rectangle I'm outlining over and over. "I went out earlier. I saw them. I went down the back steps. Go check my tracks, if you don't believe me," I say as if I expect him to challenge me, but he doesn't.

"They're beautiful," he says and shakes his head, small drips flying from his hair. "Flowers blooming in the snow."

"Now and at the hour of our death," my grandmother says then and sighs. "Flowers don't bloom in the snow. It's hard enough to coax a garden here at all. Not like it was back home in Rathpeacon even in the winter."

My father says, "Please, no Rathpeacon before coffee."

"Tea," my grandmother says and bangs the spoon once hard on the rim of the kettle.

"Coffee." Fistedly, forcefully, Dad rubs his eyes as if he wants to will himself awake into a new life.

"Flowers," Danny says. "It's magic."

"Let's go see them," I say and push him so I can follow him, slap-dash, out to the still-white snowbank where indeed flowers poke up from the drift, and we bundle them into our arms and bring them inside.

Grandma snatches one. "Cut. Cut on the diagonal. They're not rooted."

"But it's still magic," Danny insists as if he can seduce us with his faith.

Grandma glops a glob of oatmeal into a bowl, her too flowery, free-with-the-purchase-of-a-box-of-Duz china. "No more nonsense," she says. "Eat. It's good for you. It'll put meat on your poor bones."

"It'll put glue on my poor bones," I say.

"Don't disrespect your elders," my father says half-heartedly, cinching his robe.

"Grandma, it's magic," Danny ignores all of us. "Fairies. Maybe fairies planted them."

Grandma looks at the gummy well of the spoon as if it had just spoken to her. "Pah," she says. "But true back home some say the sidhe have powers. They get livelier in winter. But to be sure now and I've never seen one."

"You think they're real?" A sprite-light beams in his eyes.

"No. I can't say. Some believe. I don't know. I've never seen one."

"Have you looked?" Danny's face flushes carnation red.

"Maybe as a young girl in Rathpeacon . . ."

And at the mere name my father interrupts with a groan.

It snows all day and night, a snow that intends to stay around for a while, a snow that casts a sequinny light like a magic spell in our dark home. A snow that tingles into the room, a prickly excitement. I can't sleep, but then I have a restless heart, a mission. In predawn darkness, I watch my brother sleep. He murmurs, and I pluck the cotton balls from his ears and shove them under his pillow. He rolls away from me. I raise the venetian blind, inserting my fingers between the slats so that they won't clack. As I stare out the window at the twinkly white caught in the street lamp's beam, I think of my mother's gaiety, how she clapped her hands as if the world had been plunked down just to amuse her, as if composers had notated their music with her in mind, as if grass grew for her, as if skies glittered with snow expressly to please her. Sometimes in my dreams I walk into her bedroom and shake her shoulder, saying, "I'm hungry, Mommy. I'm hungry." And she, smelling of Breck shampoo and clean sheets, mumbles sleepily, "I can't get up yet, honey. I have no legs."

"Hug me then," I say.

"But I have no arms."

"Love me then," I say.

"With all my heart."

And the dream, always the same dream, passes out of me like the breath you hold in for the duration of a kiss. I grope my way from the bedroom into the hall where the darkness sifts down on me like Mrs. Murphy's ashes. Light, I need light, even more than sleep.

In the kitchen, Danny dances clumsily in his red rubber boots, clutching carnations to his chest. "I knew it. I knew it," he sings. "I knew there'd be more. I knew they'd come back."

Grandma quietly disappears and returns with another vase, the red boot. She rinses out the dust with tap water. She jabs Danny's new bouquet into the vase, shaking her head as she adds it to the others on the table, six of them now, bright red and pink and blizzard-white, their pom-poms nodding above the oilcloth that safe-keeps Grandma's rainy-day dollar stashes. "No good can come of this," she says and goes out and gathers the laundry, iced so stiff that it appears she's collecting a group of very skinny people. She bangs back into the kitchen and slides the frozen shirts and nightgowns and denims like pies into the wide gas oven door to warm them slowly dry. She mumbles the Hail Mary.

Danny drops his face into the green perfume of the carnations. "It's amazing, Janie," he says. "Wouldn't you love to see one? A fairy?"

"I don't know about fairies," my grandmother mutters. "Imps, more like it."

My dad carries his dishevelment, his untucked shirt and unsnapped boots, into the kitchen. "I'm walking over to Carey's for doughnuts, Janie. You feel like a walk?"

"I do."

We scuffle through the unshoveled snow, our feet guessing the lie of the sidewalks below. We pass the bookstore, its panes dog-eared with tufted snow. We pass Cannon's pharmacy. Mr. Goldfarb is sweeping the sidewalk outside his florist shop. I lower my eyes and plow ahead.

"Hold up, honey," my dad calls, so reluctantly I slow.

"Hey, Dan. Mr. G.," Dad calls, "isn't this snowstorm something though?"

Mr. Goldfarb shakes his head, his eyes mournful as Grandma's china dog's. "It's something," he agrees. "Something expensive. Think of the heating bill." He claps his hand to his forehead.

Dad pauses. "Is business bad?" Now that his own fortunes have worsened, my father listens attentively to others' troubles, their setbacks and ailments, in sympathy, perhaps, or for coping tips, or perverse pleasure. I toe my boot in the snow.

"Bad? I can tell you bad. All week the truck comes and leaves my carnation buckets like always, and all week some thief steals a bouquet. Bold as that. Right on the sidewalk. What is it with this new world? They take an old man's flowers and don't pay. What, I got no bills? You call this a world?" He shakes his head.

I can feel my father's silence handle me, the question unposed because it contains its own answer. I hear the rustle as his wallet opens, and he slides out money as quiet as snow falling.

Mr. Goldfarb stares at my father. "So why should you buy this thief flowers? You know this thief maybe? What, he put you in his will?"

And I raise my eyes to see my father hush Mr. Goldfarb by closing his hand for him over the bills in his palm, to see Mr. Goldfarb nod, disappear then into the store and return with a bunch of daisies which he shoves at me, saying, "No nothing for nothing."

My father nudges me to accept them.

"Thank you," I say, ducking my head before all their staring yellow eyes.

My father continues walking, and I fall into step. He turns once and waves at Mr. Goldfarb, then resumes his walk, the earflaps of his hat swaying side-to-side like a basset's ears, his silence reproving me. I wish that he would say something, anything, slap me, yell at me. But he says nothing, nothing when he picks six doughnuts from the jar, nothing while he pays Mr. Carey, nothing while he leads me back out to the street. As he walks, he balances the sack of doughnuts in his hand as if he's counterweighing it. The brown paper blots with grease.

He says nothing until we are home. I'm hardening myself, packing myself into a cold, small ice ball.

"I want to talk to you in the living room," he says.

I'm glad that he doesn't choose the kitchen, because I couldn't bear the cheer of the carnations now, the ruddy eagerness of Danny's face, Grandma's penitential round of kitchen duties. In the living room, in the darkness that I hate because I'm starting to think of it as home, I meet my father's eyes.

"Are you going to hit me?" I ask.

"No. Of course not. But why, Jane? Did you need the flowers so much?"

"Not me, not for me. It wasn't that."

"For who, then?" he asks. "For what?"

"I just wanted something pretty, something magic." My face feels wet, and I realize that I'm crying in the way that I dimly realize in unbearable dreams that I am dreaming.

"Magic, Janie?" He sits on the very edge of the vinyl recliner as if his body doesn't know where it wants to be. The upholstery squeaks.

I nod. "I didn't think about what I was doing. I'm sorry."

"It was a bad thing to do. A bad thing to do to Mr. Goldfarb."

"But I didn't mean it to be bad." The words tumble. "I meant it to be good, good for Danny, good for you, even Grandma. A surprise." And now the knit collar of my shirt is wet, too, the dampness wicking down from it in a dark bib.

"Don't cry," my father says. His arms fold around me, his voice a stream, saying everything, saying nothing. "I know. I know. Good, and bad . . . bad and good just flipping over and over. Life is like that." His heart beats against my ear like the sound of cards shuffling together, a magician's trick. "Jane," he says, taking my sin as his own, "I'm not doing a very good job since . . ."

But he doesn't finish the sentence, the words a disappearing act. My mother. Her voice. The memory of a voice. A dream. A memory of a dream. This is how the world releases us.

During the week, the water in the vases grows murky, the stems soggy, flabby with rot. One by one, Grandma tosses the bouquets in the bin. Every morning, Danny checks for flowers, but the fairies don't return. Sometimes when Dad has a little folding money, he buys carnations, and they pop up like surprises on the oilcloth.

Years later, after Grandma dies and we move into a house with many windows, many years later, after Dad dies and Danny is visiting me in my apartment, his feet propped on the stool while he sips the snowy foam of his beer, he looks up at me and asks, "Do you remember that year, that strange time when the flowers appeared in the snow for a week or so?" He snapped his fingers. "Like that, they stopped coming."

And for a moment I don't remember, but then, I do—all of it— the smell of Grandma, the smell of her cooking, the fading smell of my mother's hair, what Danny looked like sleeping when he was just seven years old. All of it returns. I nod. "Yes, I remember. They were beautiful, red and pink against the white, white snow."

"Did you ever wonder about that? Where they came from? Where they went?"

I don't wonder, of course, although I have suppressed this memory for years, cowering from my sin. A thief, Mr. Goldfarb called me. I intended only to be a borrower, a borrower of the flowers' grace. But it went amiss. Intent melts like the lace of a snowflake on a fingertip. A passing thing in a world heated by consequences.

"Where did they come from, do you think?" Danny asks.

I struggle, wanting now to do the right thing, the exactly right thing. I open my mouth, urged by my conscience to speak the truth. I see the little thief scuffling down the walk, grabbing a bouquet and squeezing it tight enough to strangle, tight enough that even now my throat constricts. Danny stares at me. I shrug and know in an instant that I will not steal again, not now, not from him. "Who knows?" I say and preserve the moment, frozen on memory's fingertip.

"Magic. I guess. That's all we'll ever know." He hesitates, then says, "For a long time I thought that florist on Main Street might have brought them by. You know, because Mom had died. He was fond of Dad."

I nod. Danny shakes his head, then tilts his mug, frosting his lip with an evanescent mustache of froth. It's there. He flicks his tongue. And then it's gone.

Foster stands by the window of his apartment, the tails of his Mexican shirt just barely covering his ass, and smiles at Sherry. Watching him, Sherry thinks how much he looks like Tim, her son, at four, when he weedily spiked up out of his chubbiness but didn't yet mind her watching him dress.

"You look cute," Sherry says. She slides into her own shirt, a black western one with red satiny roses on the slash pockets. "We could trade shirts," she says, slowly closing the pearl snaps.

She watches Foster stroke the creases and tucks of the bibbed wedding shirt while his eyes finger the red roses on her breasts. He hesitates long enough for Sherry to skid into his train of thought; Foster's obvious, easy to read. He doesn't want to part with something personal. He's probably heard around the Tottery Barn that she's off-balance. The bartender there used to say she had a voodoo bloom in the iris of her eyes. She stares at people too long and too hard as if she's memorizing them.

Foster's fidgeting; he feels that he should give her something to seal his gratitude. She's a good lay, he's thinking, a damn good lay. His eyes flit, light on a wagon wheel ashtray, but Sherry doesn't smoke. She follows his eyes. There's his model of a Pierce Arrow; she imagines him, giddy on the oniony smell of airplane glue, taking days to assemble it. He wouldn't part with that for his body-double. She watches him spot the penlight, consider it. It's small and purse-sized like Sherry. He can probably imagine it rolling around in the bottom of her shoulder bag with tubes of lipstick and linty tampons, her flicking the light on to locate the lock on her trailer door. He grabs it, depresses the little white button. The bulb's dim like Sherry's usually bright eyes. She sees too much.

Foster smiles at her again, but the smile is tremulous. She's sitting cross-legged on the edge of the sofa bed, shameless, rose-
breasted, dressed only in her shirt. In his eyes, the light's value
buds again with its feeble glow. No, he's thinking, he can't bear to
part with it. She watches his struggle—it might come in handy; he
could keep it on the dashboard of his truck. But he knows he
should give Sherry something to thank her, and she's watching
him with her second-sight, her sixth sense.

So he crosses the room to her perch on the mattress, uncrooks
her legs and eases them apart, stands between her thighs and
unsnaps her shirt, leaving just the bottom one closed. "This shirt's
too pretty for you to give away," he says. He wedges his fingers into
her, a vee disappearing into the black cirrus wisps of her pubic hair.

Sherry moans, strains her legs wider apart as Foster leans over to
kiss her shoulders, knowing that she should accept what she's being
offered, because she has just realized in the same instant as Foster
that he won't be inviting her back to his apartment again. She grabs
his hips and yanks him forward maybe just a notch too forcefully
for passion, and she tilts her forehead hard against his muscled,
fuzzy chest. When love is impossible, lust is its own penance.

A few golden leaves drift idly down. October strips itself down
to an essential solitude, the bare rough branches of a maple tree
raised, pleading.

Sherry is sitting out with Dona on the little redwood-stained
deck attached to their trailer. Sherry thinks of it as "the camp,"
because it doesn't trail anything, an immobile, not a mobile
home, resting on a cinder block foundation. Sherry calls things as
they are; she's a woman who knows the difference between screw-
ing and making love, between a trailer and a camp.

Peter, their landlord from Connecticut, bought the place for a
hunting camp. He doesn't raise the rent seasonally to attract
Killington skiers; it's a good deal. She and Dona have to vacate
only during deer season. During hunting season, Dona usually
stays at her ex-mother-in-law's on Pine Street while Sherry rents
a room by the week at the Sundown Motel. Dona's always as
grateful to escape the greasy doughnut smells and recriminations

of her ex-mother-in-law's as Sherry is to escape the wet Pampers steaming in the parking lot dumpster and the odors of hot-plate cookery of the public assistance makeshift families who overstay and overflow their motel rooms. All those tough kids scrabbling on the blacktop and throwing gravel at the cars passing on Route 7 make her miss Tim. Motel's a misnomer, too; the Sundown's a waiting room for life.

Dona tugs her red skirt up and wraps it around her thighs to catch more sun. She kicks mildly at Dustkitty, the cat she inherited from her failed marriage.

Sherry looks at her and laughs. "You look like you're wearing Capris in one of those old Doris Day movies."

"Mmm." Dona angles her face up toward the sun. She lives for light, won't squander a ray of it. No one would mistake her for a Vermonter. Her dark skin and black snaggy hair. It's a wonder that her family lost their way up here. But Sherry's grateful. Without Dona, her days would be unbearable. They work together at the shopping plaza, Dona at Shear Delights; Sherry at Give Pizza a Chance.

"So is Foster any fun?" Dona asks.

"You taking notes for future reference?" Sherry squirms to avoid a plastic thread that's worked loose from the lawn chair's webbing and is pricking her calf.

"No, I'm too busy home wrecking with Jerry," Dona says. "Just curious."

"Actually, he's a worrier, one of those men who's always leaping ahead to the demands he's afraid you're going to make of him."

Dona nods. "He's divorced. They're all like that."

"He has nice impulses though," Sherry says, remembering him fondling the penlight, "just no follow-through." She pauses. "They think I'm a witch, all those guys who hang out at the Tottery. It's just that if you watch men closely enough, you can understand anything, even the moment they want you to leave. It's when they're the most affectionate."

"Forget him," Dona says, readjusting her skirt. "Foster's been a womanizer since he joined AA."

Sherry scratches her calf lazily. "Yeah, they tell you at AA you've got to fill that spiritual gap with something. With Foster, it's women." Sherry's observed that AA people never give up their alcohol obsession; it just turns negative instead of positive. They're always thinking about alcohol. Alcohol is still their social link. Like Pod people, they recognize each other, hang out together. It's more Alcoholics Unanimous than Anonymous. Sherry makes it a rule not to date AA men; Foster was an exception.

Foster's irresistible when he wants to be. Women respond to his thirst for them. And she's not really certain that it's just since he joined AA. Back when she and Dona used to waitress at the Tottery Barn, Foster was hooked on both—Jack Daniel's with a skirt-chaser. Sherry giggles.

"What?" Dona asks, turning from the sun. "What?" She flattens her thighs against the red enamel shell of her chair.

"It's just that when I was drinking, you know, it's possible I slept with Foster and don't remember."

Dona grins back at the sun. "He wouldn't remember either."

But they say simultaneously, "Yes, he would." They laugh together.

"Men always remember," Sherry says. "Even drunk, they notch their bedposts. Don't you hate that?"

"Yeah," Dona says.

They fall silent in the sun. Dona turns, studying Sherry slyly. "How many men do you think you've been with?" she asks.

"In my life?" Sherry asks, astonished even before she counts.

"Yeah," Dona says, challenging.

Sherry's eyes shift up and to the right like she's counting the number of letters in Mississippi without using her fingers. She tries to cheat by advancing her tongue along her teeth one by one as she runs through the names of former lovers, but she realizes she's had more men than teeth even if she included her baby teeth. She brays a laugh.

"What?" Dona says again. "What?"

Before the sun slips to the shadowy side of the camp, Dona's gotten out bridge pads and pencils, and the two are laughing, keeping score as they list former lovers, making jokes about finesse, rubbers, taking tricks. And Sherry's confounded, genuinely confounded by how many partners she's had whose names time and alcohol have simply erased.

Sherry likes living in the camp. It's small and easy to keep up and near enough to the plaza, so that she can bike. Since she lost her license, she has to walk or hitch to work on the days her schedule doesn't coincide with Dona's. When Sherry stopped waitressing at the Tottery Barn to have Tim, Dona went up the mountain to tend bar at Amanda's. When Dona first started working at Amanda's, she hoped to meet a meal ticket, a wealthy skier, a businessman. After a year, she'd have settled for a bus ticket. She met plenty of men, but nothing clicked. As Dona often quipped after making Sherry laugh the first time, "Good sex is holy. Bad sex is ass-holey. If you can't have good sex, skip it wholly." Dona added the last line after she'd married and divorced Billy, the manager at Amanda's. In the seventies, Dona hoped she'd meet someone from out of state who'd light up an exit door. In the eighties, after the divorce, she realized she could kick the door open and the lights out herself. She enrolled in the College of Cosmetology, got her hairdresser's license. "Cosmetology. Comet-ology. Kismet-ology. Hair was in my stars," she said. Dona, like Sherry, enjoys word play.

As far as Sherry's concerned, Dona's the real thing like the ads used to say about Coke before all the nonsense about Classic Coke and the new formula. Dona's classic. She and Sherry have known each other since grade school, since Dona's parents opened Zambinos', on Allen Street near the hospital, a medical supply store that sold sad mortal necessities—prosthetics, wheelchairs, bedpans, rubber patches to keep life's retreads rolling. When her parents retired and moved to Florida, Dona stayed on in Vermont, becoming, over two and a half decades, Sherry's closest friend. As Dona commented one night watching a rerun of *thirtysomething*, the weirdest thing about these yuppie people, and there was plenty weird about them, was that they all stayed friends, all stayed in the same neighborhood. It was that way with her and Dona, but there were only two of them. They hadn't even talked about attending their twentieth high school reunion at the Holiday Inn.

In high school, Dona was really smart. She won all the lit awards for poetry. She went to Castleton with Sherry for a while, both English majors, but Dona only attended for two years because she couldn't afford more. Sherry dropped out during the second semester of senior year to work with Dona at the Tottery, until the third trimester of her pregnancy, which Dona referred to as Sherry's rematriculation. Dona had a way with words.

Sherry used to egg her on to become a writer, but Dona mocked her, "Yeah, and become one of those pathetic wanna-be's who sing into invisible microphones in front of their steamed-up bathroom mirrors. I can just picture me typing off-key novels on my air keyboard. Soon to be a minor motion picture. No thanks." That's how smart Dona is; she's beyond it. Sherry calls things like they are, and Dona sees them like they are, even the things beyond her field of vision, out there rimming her future. Dona's a realist. She cuts hair.

On the Tuesday after Sherry went to bed with Foster, Dona drives her to the plaza. They strap Sherry's ten-speed onto the bike rack first, because she'll have to bike home. Their schedules don't jibe. The October frost has tatted a crinkly doily of ice on a shallow puddle. Sherry taps it with her toe.

"We won't be sitting out in the sun much longer," Dona says. She rubs at a tread mark smudge on her pink hairdresser's smock. The femmie smock's required at Shear Delights. Dona's civvies favor dramatic contrast: red against black like a scarlet tanager, or white and black like a loon. She hates the uniforms. "I'll miss the sun." She sighs. "Okay, Sherry, let's roll." And they bump out in the Civic onto the washboarded dirt road.

When they cross West Avenue, Dona asks, "Isn't Foster's apartment near here?"

"Yup." Sherry checks her blusher in the rearview mirror.

Dona squints at her. "You think he's handsome?"

Sherry shrugs. "Do you?"

"He has nice hair," Dona says, pauses. "I know it's a dangerous question, but do you think he looked better when he was drinking?"

"I think he looked better when I was," Sherry says.

Night biking. Sherry bumps onto Cold Creek Road where it turns to dirt, and the streetlamps queue up with lengthening expanses of darkness between them. As she bikes, she plays a game that she's played since high school, searching through her mental dictionary for adjectives—tonight, words like *interstitial, intermittent,* to describe the feeble yellow flares that illumine the roadside with inverted cones of light. She bumps along to the rhythm of the words, the whir and chink of the bicycle chain, the clank of the loose front fender. Sometimes between streetlamps and on the curves and inclines, she navigates wholly blind for minutes at a time. She thinks that this is what it was like when she was drinking—navigating blackouts, her brain cells flashing briefly as they died, a firefly's sporadic green illumination, then an unmarked flight path through darkness. *Intercurrent,* Sherry thinks, *interdependent, interruptive.* A streetlamp candles above the crest of the hill. Bats flitter in and out of the wedge of light where the insects congregate.

Entire episodes of her life have disappeared, leaving spaces like those between streetlights, like the papery spaces between book chapters or the cut-to scenes in TV serials when your imagination's supposed to supply instinctively the missing scenes, the continuity. Fill in the blanks. But what if the missing filler between her memories was where she had truly, fully lived her life? Scary thought. She pedals faster toward the light.

Sherry's memory of her pregnancy has abridged itself like that; she remembers the ride to Planned Parenthood in Dona's orange salt-rotted Vega. She remembers sitting in the plastic chair in the lobby, waiting for her pregnancy test results, how tense she was, how, even then, Dona had made her laugh when she commented on the obese woman in the muumuu who was waiting for her own test results—"Sex should be illegal for some people"—how she'd regretted the laugh later, when the woman confided to them that she had a tumor not a baby growing in her stomach. But they were nervous; they'd have laughed at anything, anyone. Sherry remembers all that, but not the episodes on either side—what had she had for breakfast that morning? What had she worn? Had she cried when the counselor asked her if she was married?

And she can't remember the pain of labor or the pain of deciding not to have the abortion. She doesn't remember telling the registrar at Castleton that she wouldn't finish the last semester of her senior year, but she remembers telling Dona that she had decided to have the baby, explaining, "I know I'm not a good Catholic, but even a bad Catholic is a Catholic for life."

And Dona finally stopped arguing with her, remarking, "I guess that's one of those truths, like men preferring long-haired women; it might be untrue, but it's generally accepted untested."

Dona didn't come to see Sherry in the hospital when Tim was born, but she came and stayed with her four and a half years later when the social welfare people came to take Tim away to live with his father's parents. After the accident, Sherry was deemed an unfit mother. Tim's father wasn't deemed fit, either. His drinking had cost him his mechanic's job. His parents had initiated the custody suit. They were raising Tim and didn't permit visitation.

Sherry passes the streetlight. In the blind again, she can tell that she's advancing by the chink, chink of the chain and the whispery rub of the tire against the loose fender. By the banging in her chest, she knows that she's chugging up the hill where neglect has reforested the unhayed farmlands over the three decades that she's lived near Rutland. Her front tire grabs loose pebbles and spurts them sideways with rubbery squooshes. In blackout darkness like this, Sherry thinks that she could be anywhere. She wishes that the moon would brighten, but it's an early crescent, a dim bulb, like Tim's old Batman night-light.

One of her squeamish dreads is biking through roadkill, the tires bucking over a dead hump, soft, then crunchy, of a raccoon or a porkie. Sometimes biking to work in the morning, she sees skunks trundling out of the ground fog, or great porkies slouching along like sloths, sharp, suspicious fox-faces flashing, or the bandit faces of raccoons. But, by night, they're unidentifiable—the hump in the road, the green-eyed glint of nighttime eyes. The unpursued thought. The lightning bug.

Interval. Interlude. Biking by second-sight, she knows that she's nearing the camp. The night pales slightly where the road curves out of the woods, picked a shade lighter by the moon's crescent fingernail shaving off a parchment-thin sheet of darkness, isinglass from mica.

The chain chirr-chirrs a cricket's song. Her brakes tighten in reflex. She hears the owl hoot, and, before she hears the rabbit, she feels the flurry and squeal in her heart. Her feet resume cycling, calming her heart: the owl is only being an owl, the rabbit a rabbit. But talons find the soft spot on the throat, and the raptor's beak rips out the rabbit's voice. All unseen. The silence jets true black in the wake of the squabble. Her chain whirs faster. Somehow hearing the rabbit die without being able to see it makes it more horrible.

The chain around Sherry's heart clicks to a stop as she drops her bike in the driveway behind Dona's Civic and heads for the yellow rectangle of the door. She hesitates a moment before entering, stares at the cozily lit louvered windows of the camp. Something troubles her, a memory that's slipped through the cracks, the night she went to tell Rory that she was pregnant and stood on the sidewalk outside his parents' tidy Cape on Stratton Avenue. As she peeped in on the interior-lit Priscilla-curtained window, that window illumined her hope and her dread. Family life contained and constrained. She hadn't knocked on the door, had walked home alone, had informed Rory of his impending parentage and released him of obligation by phone. The memory, like the salty, wet ash smell of a burned-down building, makes her eyes sting. She bangs through the cat-tattered screen door. Dona's sitting beneath Connecticut Pete's mounted buck's head, her eyes rolled back white as the deer's must have been before he died, before the life flared and guttered, before the taxidermist mounted the Ginny Doll glass eyes in its sockets.

"Jesus," Dona says, clutching at the afghan, "you scared the hell out of me. I didn't hear you come up."

Sherry takes in the scene, the empty cardboard pint of Cherry Garcia, the afghan spun around Dona like a chrysalis, the blue TV light sifting over her face. "Jerry?" she asks. Jerry's the married man Dona's been seeing. She met him at Shear Delights. He came in for a trim, and Dona persuaded him into a whole new cut.

"Yeah. Damn him. Damn her, too. He's back with his wife." She shrugs. "Who gives a damn. They both have weird hair."

Sherry sits next to her on the saggy, sectional sofa. "You okay?"

"Yeah. It's just like I seem to live my whole life ten years too late.

Like I should have skipped college and waitressing entirely and gone immediately to cosmetology school. Like I should never have married Billy or, at least, should have divorced him sooner. You know what I mean?"

Sherry slumps against Dona's shoulder. "Sure, my life would be way different if I'd gotten into AA ten years earlier."

"I'm sorry," Dona says. "I didn't mean to dredge up bad memories. My troubles are feeble next to yours. It's just why didn't I see it coming? A married man. He just wanted a little side dish. He never really intended to leave her. How did I miss it?" She twists her hair into a tight chignon.

"It's amazing what can go on behind your back even when you have both eyes open."

"Yeah," Dona says. "The liar. He told me they were already separated; he never even moved out of the master bedroom." She lets her hair drop back onto her shoulders. "I'm not going in tomorrow. I called in sick."

Sherry nods.

Day biking. Ground fog's curling up like the earth's talking with warm soft breath on a cold day. Chirr, chirr. Fog is nighttime intruding into daytime. It's just a different color of blindness. From blackout to whiteout, whiteout like a blizzard's indifference or the Liquid Paper secretaries daub on their errors. Sherry wishes that all mistakes could be so easily corrected. The telephone poles and streetlamps loom surprisingly black in the wet whiteness. The fog camouflages everything until it springs out in close-up—a pine tree, an illegally dumped gas stove on the roadside, a blue squawk as a jay startles. Biking through the fog, Sherry feels wan, invisible in protective coloration. Chirr, chirr. She closes in on the intersection that links Cold Creek to Allen Street. She bumps past the stop sign, which emerges a pedal cycle too late from the fog. Red on white, a wound on snow.

She hears the idling truck before she sees it; it's running rough. Idle. Cough. Die. When the driver emerges, when she recognizes him, she considers yawing hard on the handlebars, veering right, cycling back toward the camp. But then she would be late setting up for the lunch crowd at Give Pizza a Chance. And it's too late; she's already seen Foster's face registering its slow, then startled recognition of her, its ruddy apology. Fully dressed in his journeyman's jumpsuit, his name embroidered in red on the pocket, he looks more naked to her than when she last saw him. She respects nakedness, so she brakes the bike, and with her careful eyes appraises him, the disabled truck, the Triple A sticker on the window. AA or AAA, Foster's needy.

"Hey," he says offhandedly, then adds as if he's just recalled her name, "Sherry."

"Hi," she says, bracing the bike frame between her thighs.

He doesn't get back in the cab, asks, "How's it hanging?"

She ignores the grace question. "Car trouble?" she asks. "Truck trouble?" she corrects herself.

"Yeah," Foster says. "It's embarrassing. The electrical stuff I know inside out, you know, from working at Costa's, but engines . . ." he trails off.

Sherry dismounts, and stands, holding the handlebars.

"Missed you at the AA meetings," Foster says.

"I quit about a month ago."

"Why?" Foster asks. "You backsliding?"

Sherry smiles. "No, forward-sliding. When you really stop thinking about drinking, you can stop thinking about not drinking. I'd been going eight years. I'm free and clear now." Pointlessly, she kicks down the broken kickstand, then leans the bike against the rear bumper of Foster's pickup.

"I've only been going for a year now," Foster says.

"I know," Sherry says. "The first one's the hardest one." She gestures toward the truck. "You mind if I take a look?" She doesn't want to embarrass Foster; men can be testy about their cars, their mastery of its inner workings.

Foster shakes his head.

Sherry pulls open the cab door and pops the hood, props it up. She twirls the nut on the carburetor, flutters the butterfly valve with her finger. Then she paws through her purse for an emery board and seesaws it over the battery terminals' connections. "Sometimes your battery's good, but a little corrosion keeps you from a making a connection."

Foster saunters over and watches Sherry, his hands spread on the fender. "Where'd you learn this?" he asks.

"Rory. Try her now," she says.

She hears the cab door slam. She can't see Foster's face because of the raised hood, but the engine roars, catches.

"Thanks," Foster calls. "That's great."

Sherry slams down the hood and smiles over it at Foster. "Rory's my son's father. He was a mechanic before he drank himself out of a job. I picked up some stuff from him."

She spots the penlight on the dashboard, its useful little cylinder poking up. She studies Foster's face; it's blank. She can read by it that he doesn't remember now picking up the penlight, setting it back down after they screwed, before they screwed again.

"Yeah," Foster says, "I remember Rory from happy hours at the Tottery."

Sherry wonders how much Foster knows. AA people tell stories, not to gossip, but to remind themselves: it's scary out there; it can get this bad. Sherry knows how bad it can get. Bad enough that you can climb into a car, drive down a street in daylight, sideswipe a child, and have a memory of nothing, inky nothing. Bottomless. She stares at Foster's face and blurts, "I ran over a three-year old boy. He didn't die, but he might have."

Foster doesn't lower his eyes, just says softly, "I know."

"I don't remember it," Sherry continues. "And, I can't forgive myself for this, but I'm glad I can't."

Foster nods. Sherry's staring at him with her too-blue eyes, reading him, but he doesn't seem to mind. He doesn't turn away.

"I sucker-punched a cop once at the Tottery," he says, "and I don't remember that." He shakes his head and says, "Alcohol unleashes people you didn't even know you had inside you."

Sherry smiles sadly. When Rory's parents took Tim away she felt hollow, rotten, like the burnt orange flesh of a jack-o-lantern, soul gone up in smoke. She once feared that hollowness, that empty bottle feeling of people in AA. But confiding to Foster, she realized that if you keep staring into that emptiness, eventually you stare it down. She looks up as Foster slaps the seat beside him and says, "Could I give you a lift to the plaza? It's the least I can do. We could toss the bike in the bed."

Sherry watches his face. It's clear and sharp like a twiggy branch shredding the fog. He looks happy, ready for anything—nothing more, nothing less. She may have misread him. "Okay," she says. And she climbs into the idling cab while he gets out to toss in the bike.

We met on the carnie bus. We both were midway people doing the Vermont crafts circuit. Your mystery touched me instantly. Le Bateleur, the first card, a magician confident in his skill. In your red and black hunting cap and jacket, with your acorn brown eyes and your thatchy, near black hair and beard, you strode up the steps into the bus and my life. You lugged a chain saw and dropped into place as solidly as a felled tree. Like the eleventh card turned in the spread of the Tarot, La Force, you exerted your influence, drew my eyes to you. You sat down on the seat across the aisle from me, nestled your chain saw next to you and extended your palm. Your skin felt grainy like wood. I turned your hand over and examined the whorls of your thumb, believing that, by them, I could calculate your age, count them like the rings of a tree stump.

"You are thirty-six," I said.

"Seven," you corrected.

"And you weigh one-sixty-five."

"Six," you corrected.

"I am only off by one," I said, little anticipating how much damage that an error of one could cause.

"Two," you corrected. "One twice."

"I don't do names," I said.

"Tristan," you introduced yourself.

"Triste? A man of sorrow?" I thought of Jupiter's wise but sad face above his forked beard.

But you laughed. A robust, startled laugh that seemed to take even you by surprise.

"I'm Isolde," I introduced myself, "a diviner."

"Divine Isolde," you said and slumped back in your seat.

Is Old Jones, the head of the summer carnie craft bus, jounced onto the bus in his polyester plaid pants that, from long wear, suspended a second pair of buttocks from Izzy's own. And Izzy explained the rules. "Booth rent paid up front. No drugs or whores on the bus. If you can't be discreet, don't cheat. Ten percent of all earnings funnel into my pockets." He jiggled the change in his front pocket causing the long salami, pepperoni, and string cheese he suspended from a key ring on his belt loop to sway. Izzy flipped up the pepperoni, bias-cut a slab with a Buck knife against the dash, and flipped the piece into the air, catching it in his mouth. "Any questions?" he asked, champing. "No? Then we're off."

Yelling back and forth over the tinny din of the rattletrap bus, I learned that you had no blood family that you could recall. You'd come north from the mountains of South Carolina with your chain saw. You were a sculptor, you said, a chain saw artist. You'd tired of southern pine and sought harder wood to shape. You dreamed of rock maple, of oak, of dense grains and pitchless trees.

I told you that I'd been doing the Vermont circuit for years. Izzy, my protector, both father and mother to me, had discovered, when I was a straw artist, that I had a gift for guesswork. I'd glean the hayfields after the balers swathed through, and I'd braid mats with the gleanings, weave baskets, cricket castles, and scalloped hats, birdcages and mazes hedged with miniature topiary: canaries, goldfinches, meadowlarks. They did not sell as well as corn dogs, feathered Kewpie dolls, or chameleon pins. As a sideline I linked flip-top chains, and folded gum wrappers into zigzag chains that teenage girls liked to fashion into necklaces, anklets, and belts. It was a life but not a living. Izzy would drop by my booth to cheer me up. "How many straws in that birdcage, Isolde?" he'd asked.

"About 242,500," I'd guess.

And Izzy would buy it and stay up all night on the bus unbuilding the castle and laying out the straws like some ornate I Ching pattern. And the count might be 242,499 or 501. After testing my estimates several times, Izzy came to me and said, "You cannot deny your gift, Isolde." And he sewed me the tent and painted it with moons and dragons and christened me Isolde the Diviner. Business picked up.

After we exchanged histories, you fell asleep and snored softly. When we arrived at Tannerville fairground, I set off with my gear for the midway. I read some cards, some palms, some tea leaves, guessed a weight, an age. By noon, business slowed and the tent steamed, hot with its close canvas smell, and I ducked out for a lime rickey. All the bustle on the midway congregated by the ox pull, so I strolled down. "What's the hubbub, Bub?" I asked a gawker.

He smirked. "You're the gypsy; you tell me."

I elbowed my way in, and then I understood who you really were. Your face wore a smeary mask of oil. Your bare back gleamed with sweat. In a spray of wood chips and blizzard of saw-dust, you buzzed a huge trunk of wood. Around you clustered a herd of moose, a den of black bears, giant hawks with wingspans the length of the food booth boardwalk.

The crowd clapped and chanted. You wiped the sweat and grease on your crumpled flannel shirt. You smiled straight into my divin-er's eyes, then revved the saw, hefted it, and attacked a massive block of wood. You carved a fury. Through the screen of wood dust, a bow shape emerged. Then your chain saw whirred, strung it with slender wooden strings. Dazed, you dropped the saw. It buzzed, kicking up sawdust, squirming like a live thing in the wood chips, spluttered out of gas, and died. The crowd hushed. Although onlookers would later claim that it was only a passing jet, the cal-liope on the carousel, the sound that summer makes with its distant children's voices, tree toads, and humming bees, they, if pressed to truth upon their deathbeds, would testify to what we all witnessed: the harp began to play alone. The song thrummed, high and deli-cate, liquid like strings but with the mellow resonance of wood. An arboreal sound, windy but rooted, nourished by air, earth, water, and the fire of the sun. Elemental. When the song, the trance, snapped, the crowd began to shuffle and cough and wander off. And you, Tristan, stumbled from your stupor and squatted on the ground, your back pressed against a stump.

I returned to my tent. The heat inside oppressed me. I dragged my table and chair outside to work on my spearmint gum-wrapper chains and pop-top ropes for the teenage girls. Near supper, you strolled along the midway, your hands in your jeans pockets, and I called you over. I slipped a green gum-wrapper necklace around your neck where it hung like the garland ringing Le Monde, the highest card. I did not know what I really wanted to ask. "Can you teach me that?" I whispered.

You shook your head. "Chain saws are too dangerous for girls."

"No, the secret," I said.

You squinted at me. "You can't teach magic, divine Isolde. It abides."

We shared a corn dog and a pitcher of yeasty draft in the beer tent. The midway lights were winking off the day. The freaks from the outlying towns were arriving, ogling and munching and competing for the prize of empty pockets at the ringtoss. The Himalaya whirled in its sequined, snowy lights. The rockets twirled. Fireworks rained from the skies. The Ferris wheel glittered its graceful circle. "Will you walk me to my tent?" I asked.

"I'm married," you said and blended your shadow into the night.

Izzy knew before either of us. It was Izzy's business to know things. He approached you with his knowledge. "Isolde loves you."

"Then we must find her a man, an other," you said. "My wife is a jealous woman, white hands and green eyes."

Izzy shook his head, knocked on his forehead. Later he told me, "The man is wooden, Isolde. He feels how a tree feels, sentient but not conscious."

"But his saw sings. His harp sings. And they sang for me. I heard them," I said, weaving a straw birdcage around a stringless harp.

"Illusion. Sleight-of-hand." Izzy chopped off a slab of pepperoni and offered it to me.

I shook my head and rose and looked into my hand mirror. I wondered how the diviner had neither seen nor foreseen the moment that, only with hindsight, I isolated as the moment that I started loving you. The clock's face wears blinkers. My features, the straw yellow hair, the moss green of my eyes, the spray of freckles on my cheekbones, dissolved into the silver backing of the hand glass.

You returned to South Carolina and your wife, La Jalouse. You did not know yet that you loved me. I shuffled the cards and placed the deck in the box. In September, I returned as always with Izzy to the farm where we spent the winter repainting the bus, counting the salami links and cheese wheels, going over the books, and listing the names for next year's circuit. Your name was absent from the roster. One of your hawks perched on Izzy's icebox, spreading its wings, eternally perched for flight. I did not see you again for a year, when, reopening the Tarot deck, the tenth card would drop, spinning the fortune wheel and dropping you like its ten golden coins into my palm with the jangle of inevitability.

The next summer, my twenty-eighth, Izzy woke up in his hammock on the bus from a prescient dream—choking on a mouthful of soil and the determination that I should marry that summer. He circulated word among the carnies that the man who could make me forget you could claim me as wife. Some new craftspeople boarded the bus that June. One, a whittler named Switchblade, bragged that he would be the man to claim me, but I did not trace that fate in his love line as I read his palm in my tent. And the Tarot cards insisted on Le Pendu—a destiny dangling in uncertain transition. "I will win you with my art," Switchblade insisted against the counterevidence of the cards. His voice drawled, southern-sweet and gooey. "I will win you, sugar." I examined the art at his stand—the tiny balsa wood toads, the miniature ladybugs and dragonflies. Soft wood. Lower life-forms. "I can carve angels on the head of a pin," he boasted, "invisible to both naked and microscopically aided eye."

"Difficult to prove," I said and sauntered off.

"A charlatan," Izzy said, beaming with approval.

Switchblade posted handbills announcing the advent of the day when he would steal my heart with his art. Thinking of his insects and reptiles, I scoffed. But when Switchblade finally peeled back his tent flaps, he revealed no miniature to steal my heart, but a man, a perfect man, massive in scale, but short statured, with triangular muscles like scales plating his back and corded legs and a chest staved like a barrel. His skin gleamed with the nutty sheen of golden oak. And the statue's brown eyes kept me awake at night. I tossed, kicked back the covers of my cot in the tent, steamy with the smells of paraffin and fryer grease and sweat and oil and, more faintly, the soft sweetness of summer.

Every day I scrutinized the statue, but it became only the lovelier on reinspection, yielding only one flaw—a nick, a gouge, really, the size of a quarter in the right calf. Circular, accidentally geometrically perfect. La Roue de Fortune.

Switchblade began bowing prematurely, accepting the carnies' congratulations on the impending banns. And, as the circles under my eyes scalloped like the unlit crescents of half moons, Izzy gradually conceded Switchblade had whittled himself a wife.

Then, in July, you reappeared. You drove up in your pickup, the bed hammering at the shocks with the weight of your carved wooden menagerie. You limped over to my tent, grinning. Your skin gleamed, sallow, like the moon through a fog. My fingers trembled as I wove the delicate straws into a love knot. A gust of wind puffed the straws from my table.

"And did you divine my arrival, Miss I.?" you asked with a facetious tip of your plaid cap.

"The wind heard you coming," I said and ducked, flustered, into my tent to find the broom. Before I went outside to sweep up my scattered straw, I plucked a straw from the broom. It stretched long and glossy but splintered toward the end. Hopes twinned or split? When I returned, the wind had swept all my loose straws away and you had hobbled off.

Within two days the word on the boardwalk gossiped that you suffered from a chain saw wound in your calf and, infected, you trembled, delirious with fever. I stayed away as long as I could restrain myself from going to you. Then, capitulating, I came to you with sno-cones. I supported you and held the cones to your lips. I pressed shaved ice onto your forehead and, staring at your brow, I recognized Switchblade's beardless sculpture. You. Your likeness. Your artwork. Switchblade's sculpture was yours and you. I dug your chain saw out of the tool box in the flatbed. Its gap-toothed chain matched the site of the gouge in the wooden statue's calf exactly where the downward stroke of your saw would have been timed to place it. And you suffered, feverish with your sympathetic wound, enthralled by your own magic.

I loved you with the love that lurched onto the carnie bus the first day that I beheld you, both of us blind to the destiny of love that bound us. We met in a fulfillment of the meaning of our names: Tristan and Isolde, becoming the mythic lovers that our names knew us to be. Our names refused to be denied. Once I knew that I loved you, I knew that I always had, that my life to that point was a pen waiting to write your name. That once your name was written, the ink would never dry.

I carried the chain saw to Izzy who smiled the merest smile. "So now it's done," he said. "Then we must cure Tristan."

Together, Izzy and I returned to the truck. We propped you up in the seat of the cab. Izzy whacked off two slices of pepperoni and, like a priest, placed the circles on our tongues. First, yours; then mine. When you awoke, you kissed me, and I did not know if the peppery taste burned from your mouth or my own.

That night, Switchblade, no longer able to sheath his impatience, stalked my tent and ended his hunt on my cot. When he awoke in the filtered green light of the tent, he found Carmen the cotton candy girl's black hair corkscrewing into his chest hairs. You and I were gone.

When your fever subsided, we drove up into mountains. A new fever infected us. We parked at the base of the mountain in the deserted parking lot of the ski area. You sharpened your straight-edge on a whetstone and shaved in the rearview mirror, leaving your cheeks rubbed raw and clean. I bathed in the brook. We climbed the deserted ski trail of Magic Mountain until you found the pine grove where you wished to site our bower. You spent four days and four nights, your hands tarred to the chain saw with pitch from the felled trees. You bound them together in a single pyramidal spire with saplings for ropes and strips of bark for twine.

Inside, on the mossy grass, under the blue moon, in the thin, pale, rare air of the mountains, we lay down together breathing in evergreen. Then you rose, raised me up in your arms, drank from my mouth as if I were a cup. I no longer knew if I were the drinker or the drink. The world below us receded beneath a ring of clouds. Our hands married; our lips wed. You woke between my thighs, ate berries from the hollow between my breasts. We lived naked. I cannot remember night and day, waking or sleeping, only the hardness in you softening, growing wet, growing firm again as our spire rained down its slowly browning needles and we lay together in its soft mulchy bed.

The sketchy skeleton of our shelter aspired to the sky in that summer of no rain, no weather at all until the day—I do not know if it was morning or afternoon or night—we heard their voices barking over the granite outcrops, the voices from that other fallen-away world come to call us back. As Izzy, Carmen, and Switchblade approached, you rose and pulled on your pitch-encrusted, mildewed clothes. You found your chain saw, rusty from the dew, and placed it between us on our bed of pine needles. Your sin stabbed me.

I knew you then as the adulterer you'd chosen to be—not the betrayer of La Jalouse, your wife with the white hands who'd boiled potatoes for you and laundered your plaid shirts, and neatened your bedsheets with tight hospital corners, but as the betrayer of love, our love, this love that was us but not us, too, that had compelled us up a mountain to the earthly point nearest the sky, torn us from time, and tossed us up out of ourselves. Putting the saw between us, you snapped the magic chain encircling us as if it were forged from the flimsy, folded links of gum wrappers.

As Izzy, Carmen, and Switchblade confronted us, you sat up in our bed, turned to me, where I naked lay, and said, "Isolde, it is time to go. It is my duty to return to my wife." Why didn't you struggle against duty, Tristan? Did you hear your children's voices in Izzy's, in Carmen's? You who had been ageless aged. Before my eyes, your still clean-scraped cheeks bristled, sprouted hairs, matted a full beard.

And although your ears are moldy now and no longer hear, I ask you this, Tristan. Is love responsibility? Is it the increment of daily habit reeling us into its ceaseless round of dirty pans, half-hearted promises, the unimpassioned connubial stains washed weekly from the bedsheets—only to remember that the round ceases? It all ceases. Or is it something else? The snap of a string in the balloon man's hand when a balloon tugs free and floats, rising to its element, lighter than air and farther than the field of vision? A holy, inexorable passion. Which has the greater claim? Answer me from your grave with your lipless socket of a jaw.

Tristan, you denied us.

I laughed, I crowed as Switchblade pointed at me, because he would never have me. You inhabited me, leaving no empty space for anyone else to claim. Carmen sobbed noisily. Switchblade had had his fill of her sticky sweetness. As we exited from our makeshift home, it collapsed into a pile of brush. Card sixteen, La Maison De Dieu, ruination where the nineteenth card had foretold the sun would rise on us. We were pulling against the cards.

Izzy shrugged an apology at me. "Switchblade said he would hunt you down with me or without," he said.

You marched down the mountain, a jointed wooden soldier commissioning himself to return to La Jalouse, surrendering your duty to her long, white hands. Only Izzy's tearless eyes reflected the sorrow of our descent.

"Tramp," Switchblade accused me. "Slut."

"I have lain with no man but my husband and the man of wood posed in your own tent who won me," I said and pushed him from my path. I spat on the ground and a spring bubbled up between us, cascaded down the rocky escarpment of the mountain. After that magic, Switchblade would risk no more.

You returned to your loveless, dutiful bed. I returned to the carnival. Switchblade hacked your self-portrait in oak into shredded mulch. Then he disappeared. Carmen forgave him, forgave me. Women are born to forgiveness; that is their cruelty. But I do not forgive.

I sent you letters in white envelopes, letters written in invisible ink, letters stuffed with photographs, letters with love knots woven of my graying hair. La Jalouse ordered you to burn them all, and you obeyed. Their smoke curled like incense into the sky, offering your defiance to the skies for judgment. In Vermont, I sniffed the wind and smelled my words burning, my images charred, and shuddered at the arrogance of your will. You burned my letters, Tristan, my images, as La Jalouse commanded. But no one, not even she, could scorch my memory from your hands, your thighs.

Afraid for you, I burned the thirteenth card in the deck so it could not appear upon my table. But it was a futile gesture.

You wore yourself out with duty. The white hands of La Jalouse turned black, scrubbing it into you. When at last you were dying and your will like a willow osier bent to its true nature, you sent for me. "If she will come, have her send me a note in a white envelope. If she will not, have her send a black envelope." La Jalouse would not interfere with your dying request, but she would interfere with my response.

I knew that she would intercept the note, so I sent two, identical, believing that she would destroy the first and therefore not expect the second. But I miscalculated by one day. My error of one, twice, as you once said. The second note arrived a day too late. I sent the note, Tristan, in a white envelope, and your wife with her black hands rubbed her ink into it and lay down between you and me like a chain saw. She killed you with a marriage when love would have saved you.

My white note in her black envelope read: I will not forgive you, Tristan. That is my love.

You seeped into the night, gathering like black fog into the hollows of the earth, not knowing. An unopened envelope. I hope that mold has a noble taste. I wait for my black envelope to arrive. Izzy's came. I live alone now.

And I, Isolde, live out my name, growing toothless, blind, and old in the half-moon shadows of a hawk's wood wings, telling myself over and over the story of my life until death emends it. The bony hands of the thirteenth card, reputedly, have a delicate but firm touch. Death is a painstaking editor.

Ursa Major in Vermont

From the sugar bush, from the birch stand, through the tangle of dried raspberry suckers, the bear ambled. No one was there to see the bear. The bear stood on the crest of the hill. His eyes spilled with yellow moonlight. The bear snuffled. The air, piney with frost and sharp with wood smoke and rich with November silage, wove itself into his coarse matted fur. An owl flapped by on its business. A field mouse wriggled into ungleaned hay. No one saw the bear to witness what the bear saw. Crouching on the bald spot of Terrible Mountain, the bear scuffed a patch into the frost-browned grass by the old Mansfield farm. When Mrs. Mansfield emptied her pan of dishwater in the morning, she did not pause to note the patch of scrabbled grass. She had apples to core and peel, dough to roll, pies to bake. She did not glance at the raspberry suckers who remembered the bear with fuzzy pennants of his fur, the birch stand whose striated paper curls recorded the bear's mark, the sugar bush and the slash beyond where the bear's footprints froze, tatting ice doilies in the hollows, to note his passing. The bear was back in the woods where bears come from, where bears belong. Mrs. Mansfield tossed some crabapples into the compost and returned to the kitchen. Bear in woods, cook in kitchen, and all was right with the world.

Mr. Mansfield was the first to see the bear. New moon woke him, and sound of the porcupines gnawing the salt out of the toolshed door. He tossed in his metal bed, the springs chiming against the side rails. He tried to ignore the chap-chapping of the wooden door, the cracking heartwood of branches, the skeletal clack of leaves in the wind, the rust-colored lip-lap from the old nickel faucet in the kitchen. His face itched. His thighs sweated together beneath the bunchy cotton-filled quilt. He placed the scratchy pillow over his head to shut out the dinning silence. Chap-chap. Lip-lap. He could not. He pulled on his dungarees over his flannels and grabbed his shotgun from the rack, thinking, "Damn porkies. Damn plumbing. House shot to hell."

The dark was deeper than a cellar hole. He did not see the bear at first. He sensed him. Mr. Mansfield was squinting for the porkies by the toolshed when he felt something. Like eyes, as he later told it at the general store. Just a presence. Something from away, something there. When he saw the shape hulking on the crest of the hill, not a shape exactly, more like darkness with mass, a denser shade of black, he thought that it was a dog, a coydog maybe, and he raised his gun. But two spots flared at him—green, no white, or yellow—reflecting a pale darkness. They disappeared. The hulky darkness haunched off; he could tell by the shurr and snapping of the brittle raspberry bramble. *Bear,* he thought then. His bare feet were so cold that they forgot to tell him to go back indoors to his overheated bed. He found himself staring down the darkness, down the hill. He couldn't tell you if he actually saw them, the headstones, or if he just knew they were there by memory, the way a blind man knows the feel of a doorjamb, the location of a low lintel, but, by sight or second-sight, he saw the family headstones in the pasture glint like mica in the lightless night. He lowered his gun and stumbled back to bed, fell into a half-sleep, wan and eerie-orange as predawn. In the morning, he went outside and stood on the hill where he imagined that the bear had been. The morning light tumbled yellow into the pasture. Clouds of asters scudded plum against the light. The gravestones huddled into their purple shadows. He turned, broke the skim of ice on the rain bucket beneath the downspout, splashed his arms and face with the fractured water, and went indoors to eat pie by the cookstove.

Mrs. Mansfield was the next to see the bear. In unabashed daylight. She had a pin in her mouth. Her fingers pinched a corner of the bedsheet, slightly stiff and slippery with the icy morning air. She

paused because a chevron of geese wedged themselves into her rou-
tine of chores, Canada geese honking overhead, their voices familiar, encouraging, as they nudged summer with them southward.
She raised her eyes, feeling the quick as winter sliced in behind the
geese. Soon, she thought. Green tomatoes to jar. Potatoes to the
root cellar. Quilts to air. Then she saw him. The clothespin sprang
from her lip. The corner of the sheet dropped. She bowed to pick it
up—it was tenting a cluster of asters—but she could not bend, she
realized, because her body refused to bend. She stared at her shaking hand and tried to steady it by grabbing the clothesline. But the
bear did not move. It stared down the hill. She stared at the bear. It
was over-large, like something examined too near up, and mangy.
Its lips were black. It was only about two shovel hafts from her, so
close that she could see the yellow-brown of its eyes. Later, she said
to her husband that she thought the light in the eyes flickered from
within, but perhaps that was only fanciful; perhaps they only
reflected the morning sun. But she could smell him, that she was
sure of. He smelled like humus and moss and wet coffee grounds in
the compost heap. He smelled like age and sad memories, closed up
places like cellars and attics and the closets where dead people's
clothes still hung. But she was not afraid. She was something else,
calm or something even emptier, as she stared first at the bear and
then with the bear down toward the little cemetery. But he didn't
seem to be looking at the cemetery so much as over it or beyond it
or through it, and she tried to see as the bear saw and could not,
and, when she turned her gaze back to the bear, the bear was gone.

She did not tell her husband, but she began setting out small
dishes of strawberry jam or extra pie filling for the bear. His fur
was long; it would be a hard winter. He'd need stores to get
through. He'd be bedding down soon. The squirrels were frantic
this fall, furtive as they culled and buried and scolded and stole
from each other. The mice were popping out all over the pantry
with tufts of hay and linty balls of gnawed rags. Tough winter for
sure. Haloes around the moon. Cornstalks already rattling their
ghostly husks over a snow-stubbled field. The bear would have a
rough go of it. She just wanted to do what she could. But she
didn't tell her husband, no. They didn't talk much. Their silence

had a respectable weight to it. They ate together, yes. But she'd never really been sure if they liked each other. It wasn't the sort of thing they talked about. But she knew this, she knew this much for sure—if she told him about feeding the bear he'd tell her that she was crazy, crazier than a shithouse rat, crazier than Loony Lou who lived on Dump Road. She wouldn't tell him. But she'd feed the bear sure as she set the table every breakfast, dinner, and supper. She'd feed the bear.

Full moon everywhere. The light fell, thatching the darkness with golden straws. Mrs. Mansfield was at her bedroom window pressing out a peephole in the frost with the palm of her hand. What the hell is he doing out there? She licked the pane to widen her view, and her tongue stuck for an instant to the glass. Then she felt the trickle free her tongue and she peered out, scraping the newly forming frost with her fingernails. She could see her husband clearly. And she could see the bear. They were standing side by side, or rather, her husband stood and the bear crouched, staring down the hill as the leaves scuttled like granary rats and the moon threw the dark world into high-lit lunacy. And she knew this, she knew this much even as her heart quickened with a beat that was unfamiliar to her, the way that she imagined a pregnant woman felt, the life inside that is not one's own. She knew this: her husband was strange to her. She felt about him as she felt about the bear. They were both from away. But the bear, she had not cooked for. She had not laundered the bear's bedclothes and flannels. She had not brushed the caked mud from his boots, so she felt stranger about the strangeness of her husband. She would have called the strangeness surprise if she were not a Yankee. But she was a Yankee, so she crawled back into her bed and possumed sleep until she heard her husband bang the door softly. He was inside. He was strange. While she thought this, the frost etched itself over the pane where her tongue had been. By habit, she slept.

Loony Lou was the next to spot the bear. His sighting made the bear dismissible for a while. Lou fished a lot, and he drank when he fished. More than was customary. He also tied his own flies, whimsical ones, a drunkard's flies, lime-green finches, red spiders, feathery purple umbrellas. After a hard day of fishing, he'd insist that one of his more colorful flies would reel in Yeti some day. He'd seen Yeti a week before he saw the bear, which diminished, in some people's eyes, his credibility.

He said it like this: The bear came out of the woods. First, I thought it was Yeti again. That big. But then I seen it was a bear all right. Not natural for a bear to come out by day, but he did and set down next to me no further than I am from you right now.

Some men in the general store laughed and offered to buy him another six-pack.

Lou drew himself tall with a drunkard's dignity and went on: He set there all right. Still as stone. It wasn't natural. If a bear comes to a lake, what's a bear do? He fishes. That's what. But this bear didn't do nothing, nothing but set, nothing but set and stare. Damned if I know what he was staring at. But he didn't break gaze, not even when I landed this big old lake trout. Trout was flipping all over the grass, but the bear just set there. Maybe he's a blind bear, I think. But even a blind bear can smell a fish.

"How big a trout?" Cootie asked.

Lou measured uncertainly, readjusted, six inches, twelve. The men laughed; this was rich. Lou spat in the wastebasket. Cootie offered him a Camel. Then Lou laughed, too, lighting up.

As the smoke lifted from Lou's face, Mr. Mansfield spoke up. "It's the truth. I've seen the bear." He thumped a flour bag on the counter.

"JEE-sus," Cootie said. "You seen Yeti, too?"

Mr. Mansfield didn't say anything as he left the store.

Clara Cole saw the bear next, and she was a member of the church and Ladies Guild and the cemetery committee and the garden club. If Clara spotted the bear, the bear was on the map. She saw the bear when she was surveying the new grave sites on Christian Hill. The bear was lying next to the angel statuary that marked the Howe family plot, which Clara always thought was a bit showy, those wings with all those scalloped feathers, but she kept that to herself because no one ever asked her opinion. At first she thought that the bear was just a big old dog. Dogs liked the cemetery for some reason. Maybe the bones. But that, too, she kept to herself, because even she didn't like to consider it. She thought it might be that big Newfoundland that the new family let have the run of the town (she herself had twice called the dogcatcher, but she didn't give her name) but she saw as she passed the Bewells' family plot that it wasn't a dog. The head was shaped odd—like a bear's. Only then she knew it wasn't *like* a bear's at all; it *was* a bear's, and she felt its black eye open and take her in like it was holding her there. She liked that eye about as much as she liked the yellow crow eyes that ruined the sunflowers in her garden, and she yelled, "Shoo," just like that. But the bear didn't shoo. It just held her in its one open eye, and, staying in its eye, she backed up slowly down the crest of the hill, so that the bear wouldn't know if she was coming or going until she hit the road and trotted down it to the pay phone to call up the secretary of the Ladies Guild to draft a report about the bear in the cemetery. The *Gossip*, the local paper, reprinted Clara's report and some others as well.

CONSTABULARY NOTES:
Ruth Hodds reported an apple pie stolen from her sill.

Carter Clark, who was visiting his father, William, on Mares Hill Road, reported that their laundry was shredded and trampled into the ground. A bedsheet was missing.

Kitty White reported her cat, Mittens, missing. Anyone with information can call 273–2142.

Walter Clark sighted a stray calf on Sawmill Road on Friday afternoon. He thought it might be from the Dessineau herd if Gary Dessineau wants to give him a call.

A few people commented on the outbreak of crime. Loony Lou said that it was the bear, for sure it was the bear—if it wasn't Yeti. Constable Hall got a laugh by saying, "It wasn't the bear but the beer." Still—some people felt that things weren't ordinary.

The snow came early and with determination. It was as if three seasons had converged. Asters poked up through the drifts, scattered with the last of the red and yellow leaves. The meadow of the Mansfield farm looked like a crazy quilt to Mrs. Mansfield as she stared out the window over the sink. Mr. Mansfield drank his coffee with a grim purpose. "It's cold," he said. He warmed his hands on the mug.

"Mmm," his wife assented.

"I bet people will blame the cold on the bear next. Just a bear. It's cold. He'll be hibernating soon."

Mrs. Mansfield didn't turn around. She spoke as if she addressed herself to the window. "What do you think he's looking at? You know, when he sits there on the hill."

Mr. Mansfield placed his mug on the table. "You've seen him?"

"Many times."

He knew by the way that she didn't turn around that she'd seen him, too. He stared at her back, a solid shadow framed by the golden light of the window. "I don't know. A bear stares, but I don't know if he sees."

"He looks at the family plot," she said.

"But it's just stones to a bear. Just a circle of stones." Mr. Mansfield forgot his coffee. The milk on the top skimmed into a yellow island.

"Still, it's strange, don't you think. The people in that cemetery aren't even newly dead."

Mr. Mansfield shook his head; he couldn't follow her logic. But she couldn't see him and she kept talking to the window. "I feed him. I leave him puddings, and apple filling, and strawberry jam. I feed him when I set the bread crusts out for the birds." She planted her hands on her hips, but she didn't turn around.

Mr. Mansfield felt as if some gesture were called for, as if he were supposed to rise, to go to her now, to hold her. But then he wasn't certain. He sat a beat too long and knew that the moment had passed. He stared sadly into his mug. "He'll hibernate soon," he said.

Mrs. Mansfield turned. The dishrag crumpled in her hand, her eyes unusually bright as if the sun from the window had filled them.

"What is that like, do you imagine? Hibernation?"

Mr. Mansfield shrugged. "I don't know that it's like anything."

"I think it's like a short death." She twisted the dishcloth in her hands. "That's what I think it's like."

Mr. Mansfield felt something stretch between them like light, like tight air. He felt dizzy although he still sat. "Anna," he said, but he could say no more.

"Do you think the bear is going to die?" Anna looked hard at his eyes.

"Anna," he said again, then "I'm sorry." He didn't know why he was apologizing.

He stood up. It took a long time, as if time itself were elongating. He felt very tall as his hand brushed a gray lock from his wife's face.

"It's cold," she said.

He cupped his palm on her shoulder. "I'll build a fire."

It was late afternoon, golden. The autumnal light purpled the air. Blue jays streaked over the garden. Anna Mansfield listened to the shush-shush of her feet through the snow, the soft crunch of the leaves beneath. Clouds scudded, casting perse shadows that moved like whales over the mountains. She picked her path trimly through the headstones. Ira Mansfield, 1893–1964, and his wife, Emma, whom she never met, 1895–1946. Just dates, a span of time. But she remembered Ira, remembered how he drank his coffee, farmer-fisted, how he laughed large like he couldn't contain his pleasure. He was a big man, Ira. And his daddy was buried here, too, Freedom Mansfield, and his wife, Hope, who'd moved here from New Hampshire to scrape out a life. Freedom and Hope built the house where she now lived. Not the addition, of course, that Forrest had built when they were newlyweds. She remembered the smell of new pine, the shavings curled on the floor. It smelled how? Clean, possible, she couldn't name it. But it came back crisp like the day, like the fall light. She ran her finger over the grainy granite and thought of the bear. She knew so little about bears. Did they have families? Did bears stay with their mates? Their bear seemed so solitary. She couldn't imagine him with cubs, tumbling onto him, nipping his ears. He wasn't a family bear. Her shoe toed a rabbit hole. Sleeping yet? she wondered, and she turned to climb the long hill back to the farmhouse where a plume of smoke unfurled plum-colored above the chimney against the indigo sky.

Snow fell all night. While Mr. and Mrs. Mansfield slept, the snow eddied and sifted and whirled. It went about its chore quietly, seriously, muffling fence posts and the puffy asters and the rotting pumpkins in the garden and shrouded the pines in mantles of thick white. When Mrs. Mansfield woke, her window was white. She'd overslept. She raised the sash, knocked the snow back with her hand and gazed at a world gone white as if a split sack of confectioners' sugar had been dropped by a careless baker. Now he would hibernate. She closed the window.

But the bear did not hibernate. The postmistress reported seeing him trundling through the blizzard. Wayne Dessineau said the bear was skulking around his milk shed. Chance Colebrook said that the bear was in the birch stand by the school, the old school, the Victorian one that the selectmen had boarded up. Lou said the school was haunted, but no one chose to believe him except the children who dared each other to break in on Halloween. Every year they had to replace some boards. Lou said that he thought that the bear was living in the old school, but no one believed that, either.

But they did believe that a whole vat of milk had curdled in Dessineau's dairy, and that Maisie, who never burned the doughnuts, had burnt the whole Sunday batch when for no reason at all her fryer just blew, spitting hot fat all over her new rose-trellised kitchen paper. And one of Clark's sows gave birth out of season to something everyone agreed wasn't a pig at all. It had a rat's tail and only three legs, and the sow died. And the sign on the town beach disappeared. And someone reported a deer carcass in the woods, savaged, not even eaten, just left to die, its eyes rolled white and stomach spilling out onto the snow. Carl Fisk, the game warden, went to investigate, but the carcass was gone just like that. Some people whispered, *wolves,* but others, many others, said, *bear.*

No one was surprised when the selectmen called the town meeting. But Forrest Mansfield, who had never missed a meeting, refused to go. "I see where this is going," he told Anna. "They're going to get up a committee to shoot that bear. Just a black bear. It's not some grizzly."

Anna slid a piece of apple pie in front of her husband and sat down in the plank chair next to him.

"They've got some sense, Forrest."

But Forrest shook his head and forked at his pie. "If you could only harness that stupidity."

Anna laughed. She knew that wasn't what he meant.

But Forrest was right. The *Gossip* published the minutes. The town was after bear, as if dead bear would uncurdle the milk, restore the pie, mend the laundry, and, since the meeting, Clara had kicked out her husband, Lesley, and everybody said that wasn't natural after sixty years, and they blamed the bear. And the problem was, to Mr. Mansfield's mind, that the bear was dead meat, a still target, too day-lit, too visible. No challenge in shooting a docile bear, he said to Anna.

But it was as if the bear knew. Mrs. Mansfield, lights out so that she couldn't be detected, sat vigil for her husband's vigil for the bear. Everyone had been seeing the bear, but he wasn't sitting at the lake anymore, or lolling around the cemetery, or intercepting the post-mistress, and he wasn't gracing their lawn anymore; he wasn't staring down their meadow. The snow was so deep that the foundation was banked, banked solid. A morning fire hugged the warmth inside until about five, when the sun slipped behind Terrible Mountain. They were cozy. But she knew that Forrest worried. The bear was not coming to their hill. It was cold outside.

One night, she made Forrest his special dinner—New England Boiled—only she threw in some cider vinegar and maple syrup. Forrest loved that. Some squirrels were scritching at the newspaper insulation in the addition wall, and she watched him start, watched him rise.

"Forrest," she said, "he's sleeping."

When he turned his gray face toward her, she felt his fatigue. "I've been watching," his expression told her, "I've been watching for everything—the bear, the ambush, the protection committee." But he didn't say anything, and Mrs. Mansfield wondered how she knew what he was saying, and then she wondered if she could be certain. Their habits hung like a curtain between them: known and not-known. She stood at the sink and scoured the kettle. Forrest slumped back into his chair.

He watched her bent back, her shoulders hunching as she scrubbed. "If I could," he said, "I'd take that bear by the hand and march him right into the woods, up to the ice caves where he'd be safe."

Mrs. Mansfield said something about storing her canning jars in the addition, since the space was just going to waste anyway. Then she regretted it because she thought that Forrest might think that she was lamenting, lamenting the child that they'd built the addition for, the child who didn't come. After a while, they lost hope. She started sticking the old newspapers out back, the rinsed-out cans, the broken chairs, white elephants that she intended to donate to the grange rummage sale but never got around to. She regretted all this, but, when she turned to Forrest to apologize, he was gone. Quiet filled the empty chair. The quiet felt expectant. But it was like Forrest to do that after dinner, to suddenly leave. He might fix a hinge, walk the property lines, whittle whistles for the schoolchildren. He ranged, Forrest. She wasn't surprised.

But she was surprised later, surprised, him being a Yankee and all, but there he was. In her bedroom. He mumbled something, and she thought that it wasn't what he meant—about humans being a cold breed. And he was in her bedroom, in their double, maybe quarter-sized Victorian bed, as he had been once long ago when the pine smelled fresh and his palms were creased from drawing the plane.

Forrest burrowed into the bedclothes. He said nothing, but he thought this or something like this: Anna, the bear is lost to us now. And he brushed the black hair away from her face and he remembered the yellow smell of pine when they were dizzy together, and he came to her, thinking of her and a son and daughter and son, them together. The addition. The hope, how they whispered and pillow-talked about things like errant bears and aberrant, ear-mited moose, and the bulbs that wouldn't naturalize—Anna wanted fields of jonquils, daffodils, but sometimes the ground was cold— how they talked about all this, and prayed, and loved. But the baby wouldn't come, and they became something else to each other, something strange, something you couldn't or wouldn't talk about.

Forrest knew that the foundation posts for the addition were rotting; he felt the foundation decaying inside himself somewhere, as physically as if the porkies were gnawing at his soul instead of the shed door. But he found himself wordless, naked, almost naked next to his wife, whose warmth he had not known for almost two decades. She took his hand and placed it on her hip. The flesh there surprised him. He used to think of her hips as a sugar bowl, this sweet rise, these two hard handles. His fingers kneaded into the fat. He felt a terrible doughy sinking, the mortal gravity of flesh. Desire bled from him. He didn't want her.

Anna thought: his chest is woolly and black and matted like a bear's. Anna thought, he's mine for this minute, or hour, or week. She grabbed at the withered root of him. It felt like some small thing, a cold grub. She warmed him in her hand until his breath began to catch, and she rolled over and covered his mouth with hers.

Neither rose to stare out the frost-scrimmed window. Neither rose. They were falling in love with the lost idea of each other. The morning would be difficult. Strangers hate waking up alone.

On the hill, the bear stirred in his otherness. He felt something restless move his thigh. Galaxies eddied. Stars exploded. The universe receded from the bear, who sat unremarked on a snowy hillside. The bear sat, thinking. *Bear,* he thought. Orion's belt unbuckled, and the bear felt something slip, some cincture around the world that held everything in place. He'd come back for his bowl of sweet, but the bowl was empty. He felt the night at his back. He was only a bear, an empty bowl, but, for an instant, the vast retreating pandemonium of stars was his, and he its cynosure. Bear. Universal bear. He intuited sleep, dream. The sky yawned. And the bear lurched and shambled. He returned to the woods, returning the world to its strangeness, returning to the tangle of unrecovered dreams. Mr. Mansfield mumbled in his sleep. Mrs. Mansfield did not hear him. The world turned. The galaxies swung. The turning away. The turning toward. A slow, slow turning.

❦ Tea and Comfortable Advice ❧

I'm on the phone listening to Trudy and looking out the window at her house, which is only two doors down. Trudy keeps a tidy house. A place for everything, everything in its place. She even scrubs her garbage cans between pickups. The best thing about listening to Trudy, who will keep me on the phone for an hour and a half, is that I really don't have to listen. She's reciting the list of trials that she recites every time that she calls. Chronologically: She had breast cancer, a mastectomy. Her husband, Jack, couldn't handle it, moved from their bed to the couch, then to an apartment. Now he's sporting a new midlife girlfriend. Trudy's son, Jack Junior, angry and confused, enlisted in the navy. Her daughter, Christy, heretofore a good girl and Catholic, moved into a state of disgrace and her boyfriend's apartment. The boyfriend's going nowhere fast on a Harley hawg. A grease monkey who couldn't pass the high school equivalency with crib notes and a Mensa tutor. Trudy's mother-in-law provides Trudy with her only and sorry company; she blames Trudy for Jack's wandering eye, hands, and legs. The radiation therapy is going well, no recurrence of the cancer, but Trudy's always tired.

At appropriate moments during the recitation, I offer the advice that I am uncomfortable giving: Presume he is not coming back. Move out of the suburbs. Yes, I agree with you, he *is* a bastard. The last comment discomforts me the most. I don't even know Jack Senior. In fact, I don't know Trudy.

While Trudy wonders who will mow her lawn now that Jack's gone, I look out the window at our—my—own raggedy lawn, gone literally and figuratively to seed. When I am not on the

44

phone with Trudy, I am driving my car back and forth on the forty-five-mile stretch to Philadelphia, where I teach. Otherwise I'm correcting papers in this cavernous, dark house, built in the 1920s when oil flowed slick, thick, and as freely as Trudy's story. The house, in spite of all the oil it sucks up, is cold—colder since Gene, my husband, moved out. It's more space than Yo-yo, my dog, and I need, more space than we can fill, more space than I can care for, more space than I can heat. I'm so busy freezing that I don't have time to mow the lawn.

Gene insisted we move here to the burbs. The location split the commuting distance between our two jobs—his, in New York, mine, in Philadelphia. "I'm not comfortable here," I told him when we were house hunting. "I don't feel quite right here."

"You don't feel quite right anywhere," he said.

I conceded the truth of the statement. We bought the house, a necessary concession. But when the Welcome Wagon greeted me with pumpkin muffins, plastic wallets of discount coupons and free samples of tampons and laundry detergent, and urgent invitations to join the P.T.A., the Junior League, and the Chamber of Commerce, I knew that I'd landed on an uncharted planet, and I didn't know whether I was the alien, or they were. I doubted Gene's reassurance, "You'll get used to it." Used to hobnobbing like a one-headed symmetrical geek among Hydra-headed asymmetrical geeks who wore gabardine suits and fingernail polish and applauded warmly after the first-graders warbled "Yankee Doodle Dandy" off-key? I thought not. And I doubted that I even wanted to get used to it. But Gene's advice always distilled to: "Go with the flow." I didn't go with the flow; he did.

He's living in an efficiency apartment now somewhere near Washington Square. First the commute wore him down; then my unhappiness did. I do not know if he has a midlife girlfriend. He doesn't call often, and, if he did, with Trudy humming up the wires, he couldn't get through.

At school I've forbidden my students to use the word *irony* in their lit crit papers. "*Irony* is a one-word cliché," I caution. "Explicate instead," I advise. But that one taboo word best explains my presence here. I live, metaphorically speaking, in

Irony, Pennsylvania. In the past ten years, I've also lived in Irony, New York, and Irony, New Jersey, relocating three times, each time for a man, and each time I've landed in a foreign territory where people drive oversized gas-guzzlers and shop at malls where, overwhelmed by all the choices, they return, after long malling days, with tiny, tony bags containing almost nothing: a foil-wrapped chocolate, a perfume sample, plastic-laminated paper clips—walking advertisements for the stores.

I was happier before I started following my heart—back in New England teaching at a boarding school, where people rarely drove their small, economical cars because they pulled down pea-sized salaries, gas was pricey, and there was nowhere to go worth going to, where people shopped for the few things that were worth shopping for in the Sears catalog, the local Ben Franklin's, or the school bookstore.

But I don't know if I was happier because of location or time. Ten years ago, a younger world seemed possible, brimming with alternatives, new directions. I just kept taking the road more trampled by as I fulfilled my personal manifest destiny and found myself butting smack up against the boundaries of my poor choices.

"At least I have my dogs," Trudy says on the phone.

"Yes, dogs are good company," I respond automatically and think, *it's because they have no discrimination.* But I don't tell her that. Yo-yo's been locked in the house all day. A faint unpleasant odor accuses me of neglect. She hates being left alone while I teach. She's dropped another hint, probably on one of the oriental rugs. Yo-yo's very discriminating about some of her habits. No cheap throw rugs for her doggy deposits, only the finest nap, the tightest weave will do, thank you. "A dog's love is unconditional," I lie to Trudy.

That jump-starts her. Trudy loves to chatter about her dogs.

I try not to murmur any "mmm's" or "ah's" to encourage the flow of pooch shmooze. I can imagine the stacks of papers on my dining room table duplicating themselves, dittoing their errors across reams of paper—sentence fragments, dangling modifiers—all yearning for the behavior modification of my red pencil. It is going to be a long night.

Trudy is, at last, winding down. Any minute, she'll say, "See you." What she really means is "Ring you." Trudy only leaves her house for grocery runs to the Acme, transported in her mother-in-law's station wagon. She doesn't know how to drive the Beemer Jack Senior left in the drive.

"Bye," I say.

"See you," she says.

Not if I see you first, I think with adolescent meanness and hang up. I've forgotten to thaw anything for dinner. Gene took the microwave. Yo-yo, head on her crossed paws, nose to the dinner bowl, rolls back her eyes in reproach. I dump some kibble in the bowl. She looks at me: Is *that* dinner?

"Yes, that's dinner," I say and slather peanut butter on a slice of bread that even the Acme day-old bakery would reject. Carrying my sandwich in my mouth, I drag my briefcase full of compositions into the dining room to add to the stack of compositions already awaiting me on the table. In the 1920s, no doubt, families met in this room over roast goose for holidays. Party dresses and tuxedo shirts circulated, sampling canapés, considering the dryness of the champagne or gin. And now I, with like joie de vivre, contemplate an evening intime considering the dryness of 180 adolescent imaginations suffering crises of identity and end punctuation. I have actually come to look forward to the occasional evident plagiarism; at least, stylistically, the prose improves. A long night. Fortunately, tomorrow is an early day—no faculty meeting.

When the phone starts ringing again, I resist the optimism that it might be Gene. More likely it's my department head, Joan, scheduling an emergency departmental meeting, or it's Trudy again, or a hysterical tenth-grade procrastinator. I don't answer. Yo-yo barks, impatient with me.

"Lie down," I command. "Give it a rest."

The phone rings on. In the dark, in the shadowy, lonely rooms, it sounds menacing. "It's probably Trudy's husband," I say to Yo-yo, "asking me to keep an eye open for signs of her infidelity. Yuk. He's the original wrong number." Yo-yo cocks her head at me. One thing about dogs—they have no sense of irony.

∾

When I come home from school the following afternoon, Yo-yo is sitting in the driveway, squirming.

"How did you get out?" I ask. But behind her I see the open door. I approach the back door, and, as soon as I glance into the kitchen, I know: I've been burglarized. Silverware, clothes, and old photographs litter the floor. I stoop and pick up a photograph near the threshold. It's Gene with Yo-yo as a puppy, the day he brought her back from the shelter.

"You're some watchdog," I say. Yo-yo wags her tail. I wonder if I should go inside. Someone, the burglar, might still be in there.

"Come on, Yo-yo," I say, scritching her ears. "Good girl." And I enter the dark house to call the police.

When the detective arrives, he tells me what he can about the burglary: nothing. He dusts for fingerprints. "But it's clearly a glove job," he says. "Could be anybody, a pro, a neighborhood kid with a drug problem, fencing the goods. You should get a security system."

"I had one," I say, "but he moved out."

He smiles. "I'm divorced, too. Believe me, in the long run, you're better off."

"Than what?" I ask.

He tugs at his visor. When he leaves, he mumbles an apology.

"Hey, you didn't rob me," I say, then realize that I don't really know that. As he said, it could be anybody, a neighborhood kid. Jack Junior, I wonder, but, no, he's in the navy now. Jack Senior? Almost his M.O.: take what you can, and take it on the lam.

After the detective leaves, I try to make sense out of the dumped drawers, list what is missing for the insurance company. But I know what's missing—Gene.

When the phone rings at four, I answer, thinking that it might be Gene, the police, the good hands of Allstate.

"Hello," the female voice says. "It's Betty."

I flip through the mental Rolodex. Betty. Betty. Betty from next door. Betty who hates Yo-yo because she barks at her toddlers when they terrorize the neighborhood on their Big Wheels. That's all that I know about my next-door neighbor, Betty.

"Betty," I say, "look, I'm sorry the dog got out again. I hope she left the kids alone. You probably noticed the police cars. A rude burglar forgot to close the door behind him, and Yo-yo . . ."

"No. No, that's not it," Betty interrupts. "I'm calling about Trudy. Trudy who lives next door to me, the other side."

"Yeah?" I ask.

"You know Jack left her three weeks ago?"

"Yes," I say, wondering what this is about—a block party? Neighborhood Watch committee? "I know."

"She's drunk."

"It's four in the afternoon," I say stupidly, as if lushes watched the clock.

"Yup, " Betty says, "and she's drunk. Again. She's in the driveway. I think she hit her head on the bumper of the Beemer trying to start the lawn mower. She really looks a mess. I thought you should know."

"Why?" I ask, scanning the room, the disarray of my past life: jewelry, photographs, books; that's me all over, I think. "Why should I know?"

"Because you're friends," Betty says.

"I barely know the woman," I snap. "She took care of my dog once."

"Then I'd say she's a good friend," Betty says and hangs up.

Yo-yo tilts her head at me. "That woman really hates you, Yo," I say. "Come on."

I stop to lock the kitchen door, but the tumbler spins, unengaged, a gift from your neighborhood felon. I wonder if there's a locksmith coupon in my Welcome Wagon wallet. If so, it's probably expired. "Shit," I say and kick the door closed.

Yo-yo snuffles her way down the street, and, when she realizes that we're nearing Trudy's, she starts wriggling, and bouncing, and yipping, and wagging. Trudy spoils her dogs. No kibble for her babies—chipped beef, ground sirloin, whole milk. They eat better than I do. The week and a half that Trudy watched her, Yo-yo became Bulbo, the Orson Welles of dog stars—"We will sell no 'K-9' before its time."

Gene had suggested that we take a vacation, but I couldn't place Yo-yo in a kennel without a record of her rabies shots. Gene spotted Jack Junior one morning waiting for the bus on the corner, swinging his backpack. "Hey," Gene yelled from the driveway, "you interested in taking care of our dog? Five bucks a day."

"Sure," Jack Junior said.

We'd intended that Jack Junior feed Yo-yo in our house, walk her twice a day, but Trudy couldn't bear the thought of Yo-yo's loneliness. They'd taken her into their neat little ranch house where their two dogs already fed frequently and happily, so the shepherds waged no skirmishes with Yo-yo at suppertime. In Trudy's house, the dog dish runneth over and over. Sirloin. Beef tips. I've only been inside her house once, the day that I went to pick up Yo-yo.

Jack Senior had greeted Gene and me at the door. With hammy handshakes, he welcomed us inside. The family had crowded around us in the clean, tastefully bland hall. While the four DaSilvas jabbered about what a great dog Yo-yo was, I peered over Jack Senior's shoulder into the sky blue living room, with its unwrinkled sofa cushions and unmashed carpet, as if plastic slipcovers slid between this family and the messiness of their lives. I felt as if Gene and I had blundered into a parodic dream of suburban bliss—a photo Christmas card of middle-class happiness. Two flabby German shepherds jiggled with joy, jostling against the hall table with the discreet shrine to the Virgin Mary. The dogs even nuzzled Yo-yo as we turned down the offer of tea or a cocktail, paid Jack Junior, thanked the DaSilvas and left. The memory stings. I miss Gene. I miss our snickering amazement at how the other half lived. I miss Trudy's orderly prefab family life. I even miss my snide ingratitude that day. I could afford to risk shame then. We all could. We thought that we were happy.

As we walk down the hill, Yo-yo's urinating manically on the rhododendrons and pachysandras of the Lawn Doctored yards. She pays particular attention to one of Betty Boop's new azalea bushes. Swell. The Neighborhood Watch committee's going to take out a contract on me—or, at least, my dog. By the time that we reach Trudy's gate, Yo-yo's boinging like a superball. A trickle of blood leads up the slate stepping stones to the door like the trail of pebbles Hansel and Gretel surreptitiously dropped so that they could find their way home out of the woods. I doubt that Trudy will ever find her way out; she's been in the woods too long. I wish that I could pivot, run back up the hill, call a locksmith and lock myself inside, swallow the key in a single gulp like some cartoon character. "Now you'll be safe and cozy, Auggie Doggie." But I cannot turn around. I owe this much to Trudy.

I knock. The dogs yap. No Trudy. I lift the flap of the letter drop and stare through its rectangular peephole at the dark hall.

When I had recounted my evolving acquaintance with Trudy to Joan at school, she asked, "Why do you feel you owe this woman your friendship? After all, you have nothing in common."

"Yes," I said, "that's the problem. I listen to her woes, and, at the end of her recitation and my expressions of sympathy, the friendship just fizzles out."

"Does the woman work?" Joan asked. "Does she read? Does she sew? Does she travel?"

I shook my head to each question.

"What does she do?" Joan asked.

"She cleans. She talks on the phone. And she raises her children, or used to," I said.

Joan shrugged. "Tell her to get a life."

The words rang, and still ring, very harsh. Does Joan realize how difficult that is—to invent, to reinvent a life?

I crouch, and through the raised brass door of the mail slot, I call: "Trudy. Trudy, it's Maura from two doors up. May I come in?"

Yo-yo paws the door.

"Coming." The voice sounds weak. I hear a scuffle-scuffle behind the yapping dogs. Then Trudy stands in the doorframe, a white towel, already spotting with blood, wrapped like a turban around her head. "Yes," she says, "what can I do for you?" Her face matches the white of the towel.

"Lie down. You can lie down for me," I say, stepping inside, taking Trudy's elbow and guiding her through the pristine living room. Its inviolate neatness pushes me on, definitely not the room where people pause to bleed. I escort her through the kitchen into the family room, where she was obviously resting when I knocked. The sofa pillows tumble in disarray. A glass sweats into its coaster. A bottle of aspirin spouts a puff of cotton. It occurs to me that Trudy had everything under control before Betty summoned me to her assistance.

"Let me help you lie down," I say and ease her onto the couch. Trudy's unbelievably thin, as thin as her dogs are fat, as if the love that she bestows on them is being siphoned from her corporally. Her arm feels twiggy and brittle in my hand. I imagine that it might suddenly snap like a slim branch of birch frozen to the heartwood.

Trudy reclines. Her eyes stare up at me from her swaddled head. My thoughts jam behind my tongue. I don't know how to console this woman whom I do not know. "Trudy, your house looks very nice."

Her eyes glisten. "Do you think so? I've always tried to take good care of it. Of course, it's hard now with Jack gone." Her eyes tear.

I don't think that I can bear the intimacy of her crying. I flatten my palm on her forehead. "It's a lovely home," I say, emptily.

"That's top of the line wall-to-wall." She indicates the blue shag carpeting. "We added the brick-face hearth around the wood-stove, too."

"Mmm, lovely," I repeat. It isn't, but honesty seems pointless. I stroke her almost fleshless upper arm. "Trudy, could I get you something to eat? You're awfully thin."

"Do you think so?" She perks up with vain pleasure. "Do you think so? Really? I've tried to stay in shape. Jack can't fault me there."

"Nope." I shake my head in negative agreement. I now know two personal things about Trudy, no, three: she is a daytime tippler, takes pride in her home, and is an incipient anorectic. "Trudy, I'm going to get you something to eat."

"Okay." She smiles.

The three dogs tail me to the kitchen, wiggling expectantly as I yank open the cabinets. I locate the box of dog biscuits and toss a handful to the floor. I find the soup in the adjacent cupboard between a jar of relish and a can of tomatoes. With a small shock, I realize that Trudy alphabetizes her food. How disorderly can groceries for one get? How much organization do canned goods require? I realize for the first time the profundity of Trudy's loneliness. At least I can stem my loneliness, deflect it with the activity of my commute, my work. I heat up the teakettle on the back burner, locate the tea bags in a canister on the counter. I find the saucepan and heat the can of chicken noodle. By the time that I steep the tea, find a bowl, soupspoon and tray, and return to the family room, Trudy is sleeping.

I leave the tray on the coffee table with a note suggesting that she reheat it in the microwave—Jack left hers—when she awakens. I tell her that I'll check back.

The fixed Easter-egg blue of the Virgin's glass eyes stare vacuously at me as I leave as quietly as Yo-yo will allow. I press in the lock button on the front door before closing it. It's a dangerous world.

As we walk up the hill, I turn to Yo-yo and say, "If I were Trudy, the first thing I'd ditch, after my attachment to Jack Senior, would be that Virgin Mary statuette. It's the root of half the trouble, that sexless statue, almost but not quite a goddess. No actual power, but the world still expects miracles. You have a baby immaculately then get assumed right out of the testament. Yup. I'd deep-six that virgin."

Yo-yo urinates on the wheel of a tricycle at the end of Betty's drive-way. I hope that Betty isn't standing sentinel at her picture window, but, in case she is, I give a blind false-hearted wave.

I fix myself another peanut butter sandwich, wishing that I had a can of chicken noodle lurking somewhere in my cupboard. After dinner, I run through the locksmiths in the yellow pages. It's futile; no one will come by until tomorrow unless I want to pay double time. I don't. I heave the sideboard, scraping a path on the oak floors, from the dining room to the kitchen and wedge the hutch against the lockless back door. I feed Yo-yo, pick up some more of the debris from the burglary, and settle on the living room couch to correct a few papers.

I do not realize that I have fallen asleep until the telephone's ring wakes me. Yo-yo is barking somewhere in the house. I stir, muzzily, reach for the switch on the lamp and snap it. Nothing happens. The darkness electrifies me. The phone ring feels as if it's emanating from inside me. Neural transmissions firing and misfiring. I fumble my way through the darkness and lift the receiver to my ear. "Yes?" I ask. The connection dies. I press the dead earpiece to my ear, then drop it to the cradle. By the light sifting in through the window from the streetlamp, I check my watch. Eleven o'clock. I glance down the street. Lights burn in Betty's and Trudy's. I recall a horror story about a robbery-murder. The robber entered the basement and turned off the main circuit breaker to take the resident by surprise. My legs run watery, pool at my feet, which feel as if they are sinking away from me. I cannot move them. Panicky impulses flash like exploding neon images in my dark imagination: call 911, police? Trudy? I can't call Trudy. Betty. Yes, call Betty. My fingers fumble in the drawer of the telephone stand for the bug light. By its feeble light I find the phone book, Betty's number, dial. In my jittery state, my hands belong to someone else, someone surprisingly calm, competent. But my voice betrays me. Shrill, it trebles like a stranger's.

"Betty, it's Maura, next door. I was burglarized today. My power's out, and I just got a hang-up call. I think there might be someone in the house with me. Could you come up for an instant?"

"What? Our power's on," Betty says. "Maybe it's just an outage. On the corner there, you could be on a different line."

"Yeah. Maybe. It's just I'm alone up here, and someone broke in today, and I wondered if you could come up for a minute."

"Robert's not home," Betty says. "He's at a management seminar at the Ramada, 'Taking Charge of Your Life.' I don't know when he'll be back."

"Yes," I say, "I see. But could you just come up? . . ."

"I can't leave the kids," Betty interrupts me.

The kids. I can see Betty's lights twinkling just twenty yards away. The blue aura of her TV in the family room lights me with longing. "No, of course. I wasn't thinking."

"Look," Betty says, "I'll call the power company for you. See what I can find out. If you want, I'll call the town police, ask them to do a drive-by."

An undertone in her voice sounds exasperated, slightly accusing—as if my circumstances were the inevitable fate of a woman who mismanages her dog, her yard work, her marriage, her life. Thinking of the detective who investigated the robbery, I say, "No. It's okay. Don't bother. Thanks for the offer though. Good night."

As I hang up, the lights flicker on. I stand very still, listening for unusual sounds that might betray an intruder. Wherever Yo-yo is, she is quiet. My legs recover. I think that I can move again. Then the phone jangles, triggers an afferent nerve. I answer by reflex, "Yes?"

"Mrs. Fox?"

"Maybe," I answer.

"Is this 736-2044?"

"Yes."

"This is Keystone Power. We have billing in the name of Eugene Fox."

"It's Ms. O'Connell now. But right residence."

"We understand you had a little problem with the power tonight. A transformer was out. Has your power been restored?"

"Yes," I say, "thank you for calling." When I hang up, my legs are strong. I whistle for Yo-yo. Before I can find her, the phone rings again. Now what? I answer.

"Hi, Maura?" the wan voice greets me.

I should have known better. It's Trudy. "Yes. Hi, Trudy."

"I found your note. Thanks for the soup."

She hiccups the last word: *soo-up*. She's tipsy again. I doubt that she has eaten the soup. "You're welcome," I say.

"You said you were going to check back. Do you want to come by? I'd love the company," Trudy says.

I hear a faint clink of ice cubes in the earpiece. I begin wearily, "Trudy, it's after 11:30. I have to work tomorrow. The house was burglarized today. I'm alone here." My voice surprises me, gaining volume, momentum, speed as I speak. "I know you're suffering. But we're all suffering. I'm happy to help you out as I can, but I only have so much free time. I'm coping with my own personal problems. I have problems. I have a life, too. Don't you understand that?" I end in a shout.

"Yes. I do." Trudy's voice cuts me, small, fragile and as sharp as a shard of a shattered wineglass. The phone clicks. Dial tone. I hear Yo-yo's toenails scratching as she scrambles out from under the bed upstairs, click, click as she crosses to the landing.

"I'm coming Yo," I call. As I tromp up the stairs, I realize that I'm exhausted. I strip by the bed, don't even bother with a night-gown, slip between the unwarmed sheets. But as tired as I am, I cannot fall asleep. Trudy weighs on my mind. I think of her, drunk and empty, lying on her couch, and me, tired and empty, lying in my cold bed, the two of us connected only by loneliness. And my loneliness deepens. It is not only that I miss Gene, but also that I miss me. Trudy has forced me to surrender a notion of myself. I am not as good a person as I thought myself to be. I have rammed up against the limits of my compassion. Tomorrow I will rise and start over, call Trudy, apologize, explain, resume our lop-sided friendship, but I will know that I am not the person who I thought I was.

When Gene left me the last time, I asked, "Are you abandoning me?" The question sounded quaint, Victorian.

As he loaded a carton of records into the hatchback, he turned his face toward me and said, "That depends on how you look at it. I'm releasing you. Think of it as regaining your freedom."

The Welcome Wagon ladies unfurl yards of bunting every national holiday. The P.T.A. stands allied in its mission. The Chamber of Commerce issues flag pins. Ceremonious freedom. But lying passively in the dark, waiting to forgive myself as I fail to become who I once—long ago—thought and hoped I was, I com-miserate privately with Trudy who has lost more than I. We both find ourselves haunting the rooms of our own houses, but she has lost a family.

Free of our attachments, we both founder. Freedom confers a dreadful responsibility. The alternatives remain. Free to fail. Free to fall short. Free to do everything or nothing. I pull my covers over me like a plastic slipcover, drift into uneasy sleep with this last waking certainty: freedom, pure as a vacant mirror, gleams dreamless and terrible. Under the bed, Yo-yo whimpers and scratches in a dream.

Bluebeard's First Wife

She lived in once upon a time and far away. She was content in her marriage; indeed, she thought herself fortunate. She had trunks full of white lace and satin dresses, larders full of sun-colored honey and fresh bread, caskets of jewels that she plundered to pin the topazes and carnelians, the rubies and emeralds in her hair for play. She had maidservants and manservants and a stable full of ponies and vases full of peonies and poppies, cages merry with canaries and mourning doves, a silly lapdog with a sad wrinkled snout, a cast-iron ring of clanking brass keys, and a husband who provided all this because he loved her, or she amused him—she could not be certain which. But he smiled on her when she twirled around in the morning light by the long bedroom windows, her white dressing gown billowing. She did not pause to consider if she loved him. She was grateful for his indulgence. He was older than she, her husband. But it was partly her youth, she knew, that amused him. His age did not concern her. He was a husband, likely better than most, but then she had no other for comparison. What did she know of husbands? He seemed agreeable. He was a bit stout, and the hair on his chest and forearms bristled coarsely. True, his beard was blue, which was perhaps unusual, but it was a pretty blue, the cobalt of the ocean a day after a July storm, the restless stirred-up blue that enisled their castle.

One morning shortly after their wedding, as she danced in the yellow light, he summoned her by patting the large down pillow on which he lay. "Wife," he said, "come here. I must go away for a few days."

She joined him on the bed, tucking her bare feet under her dressing gown.

"Away?"

"Away. In my absence you have sway over the servants and every liberty save this." He jangled her heavy key ring until it chimed, then fingered one long, thick key, brass the color of flesh. "This key you must not use. This key opens the door you must not open, the door, the heavy wooden door, which lies at the end of the lowest corridor in the castle. That door and only that door you must not open." His blue beard purpled with a tangle of shadows. "Do you understand?"

She nodded, and later that afternoon she watched him ride off on the spiral, looping road, traversing down to the sea until she could no longer make him out.

She dressed. She drank pomegranate tea with honey. She teased the ugly lapdog. She fed seed to the canaries from her lips. She played the harp until her fingers bled, but she did not descend the stone steps to the lowest corridor where the wooden door must not be opened.

When her husband returned, he brought her a spun glass lark that sang in vitreous chords. He brought her tangerines and nutmegs and yards of silk as iridescent as peacock tail feathers. She received the gifts with pleasure, and she was with her husband as before until again one morning he patted the bed and again he told her he must go away and again that she must not open the lowest farthest door. She nodded, but this time she, eyes to the counterpane, asked, "Where are you going?"

"I have business."

"Business? What do you do?"

"I maraud."

"You are a marauder?"

"Yes." He settled back comfortably beneath the quilt of his beard and studied her lowered face. "Is something bothering you?"

"No. Not exactly, but yes."

"Out with it then."

"I do not know my name. What is my name?"

"Name? You are Bluebeard's first wife."

First? Then she knew that her eyes must be mirrors with depthless backs and not windows with flirty curtains, because she had no name, because she was leading some sequence as yet unclear to her. Falsely, gaily she tugged at his beard. "Then I shall be Goldbrow, since my brows are gold, as you are Bluebeard, since your beard is blue."

"Your conceit is quaint, pet, but I have marauding to do." And he hefted his weight from the bed.

Again from the window she watched his departing back. And again she did not descend the stone steps chiseled in her curiosity. But she kicked the lapdog, dyed her hair black with henna, freed all the mourning doves and canaries, who flew and molted and crapped all over the silks and brocades, and she taught her harp to play alone. Then she stripped off her morning gown and ran naked down the helical path to the sea's edge, grinning at the manservants who stood on the scarp, agape, and she listened to the waves as they licked up and trickled over the ovoid stones with a steamy hiss.

With bird lime and cobbles she built a miniature replica of her castle, giving great care to the lowest, longest corridor. Her hair snaking like cords of black wind, she climbed back to the castle, ransacked the coffers, and placed gemstones in her navel, her nostrils, her ears, her mouth, her second mouth, and danced to the music of the independent harp, then sat down at her white writing desk, where she stored the sheaves of the household inventory, and rewrote on their backs all the folktales that she remembered from her youth that she could not remember, for it was lost to her because she had neither name nor memory.

When her husband returned, he brought her skins—skins sleek and jagged with charcoal chevrons, skins staring with a thousand black unfocused eyes, pelts as sleek as her woman's hair. His blue beard wrapped about his neck like a garrote.

She posed for him. She flipped her tresses. She swayed. She cosseted him, twisting the ends of his blue beard. "Do you notice anything different?" she asked.

He shook his head. "You are fair and beautiful. You are always fair and beautiful."

She tossed her head, her hair lashing her face.

"Her hair," the harp chanted, "her hair, which once was flaxen, now has grown charred and waxen. Stroke it, stroke it, if you dare, and learn what stains that once gold hair."

He glared at the harp, then stared at her batwing tresses, her pale nakedness. He shook his head and asked, "The keys?"

She dropped the ring into his lap. As canaries nested in his hair, his beard, he examined the one stubby brass key with a scrutiny he usually reserved for the rubies he brought her. "You have not opened the door," he said.

It was not a question. She hummed to the harp and danced, danced until night fluttered in the long window, danced until he fell asleep. Long after he'd begun snoring, she danced until she wore out the soles of her feet and crept into the bed. In the morning she began to wish him gone again, gone already. Surely he had more marauding to do. But he did not go. He called the maid-servants to shake out the bed linens. He opened the shutters for the birds. He cut the strings of the opinionated harp. He burned her carefully inscribed folktales. He kicked down her castle on the shingle, the toe of his boot giving particular attention to the lowest, longest corridor.

She wished him gone. She was convinced that he knew that she wished him gone; therefore he stayed, stayed with a grim pleasure, stayed until the sun bleached out her hair, until she donned her morning robe just to curtain herself from him, and then, when she found that she no longer wished him gone, that she fingered the glassy singing lark with pleasure, that she was taking careful stitches in the peacock silk, then, only then he summoned her and announced again that there was marauding to do, again with the warning about the long corridor, the locked door. She rubbed peony petals into her cheeks until they bloomed pink in her glass.

"Where are you going?" she asked, turning to study herself in his black eyes.

"Marauding."

"Marauding where?"

"Away."

"And where are we?"

"Away, too."

"What place? Where? What year? What is my name?"

"Once upon a time," he said.

She watched his departing body sway the back of a liveried mare. Who was he, this man, her husband? Was he admirable? Was he deplorable or some attribute in between—swashbuckling? Was he a swashbuckler? She wondered what the word meant. Swash, wash, buckle, iron, cinched in, buckled to the knees beneath a swashing lash. Soft sounds and hard ones. What did it mean? What did it mean, a blue beard? Privilege? Distinction? Deformity? Depravity? Her vocabulary was straining the conventions of her character's conception.

She was a fair maiden and once upon a beautiful maiden and once there dwelt and a wicked whatever and once upon the severed seven heads of the ogre's children and a path pecked crumbless by seven crow princes and a rags-poor girl without hands losing the path until the narrative finds it, locates it here. HERE:

Once upon a time, Bluebeard's first wife descended the forbidden steps to the forbidden corridor to the forbidden door and with the forbidden key fitted it oh so tremblingly, fitted it with so much anticipation, into the waiting lock. Fitted it, thinking, this is how locks like it. I've heard about this—shove it tough. Be tender; make it hurt. The brass key warmed to her touch. It rose firm toward the lock. It slid into the tight dark niche and with a click unlocked possibility. Once upon a time. In white, in a veil of darkness, Bluebeard's bride trembled on the threshold, then bold, eyes open, stepped definitively across. But what was this? What could it mean? She had known rooms lined with boxes of jewels that could blind with colored light, larders dripping with honey, redolent with anise and clove, walls lush with tapestry, beds slithering with silks. But this room. These walls. This room. It was bare.

What did it mean, this bare room? The problem with an empty room was that one longed to fill it. What could it signify for her husband? Did he intend it as a parable? That their marriage was empty? Did he intend it as a warning? As she padded barefoot over the curiously warm stone, she thought it the most terrifying of rooms, more terrifying than the room where the cook beheaded the chickens, more terrifying than her bedroom on her first night. Perhaps it symbolized her memory—so bare, so uncluttered, that she lacked one. Perhaps its hollowness resonated with her missing name. "Goldbrow," she called aloud, expecting an echo, but the room swallowed it. The key throbbed in her fist. Her husband intended it as a riddle, perhaps, some conundrum to solve as proof of love. But how could she solve it if she could not ask it? He'd forbidden her to open the door. He'd grown tired of her perhaps, and intended this as her cell. He crossed the sea for a woman, a woman with more charms, a woman with a name, Rapunzel, Rose Red, Aurora, or Donkeyskins.

The stone-walled, stone-floored room was cruel. It had neither use nor meaning. What do you mean? she asked of the room and stamped her foot. What do you mean? She tugged at her hair. No answer. So this was how fairy-tale princesses went bad. She closed the door. She locked it.

For seven days and seven nights, she endured sleepless dreams—sometimes seeing a shimmer in the corner of her eye—a procession of headless women carrying something in their bloodied aprons. But when she turned to demand of them what they meant by this haunting, they vanished. Sometimes she envisioned an odalisque naked on a bed, her husband between her thighs while she ate grapes with a bored air. But the odalisque, too, disappeared before the wife could pose a question. Sometimes she saw her husband's anger crowd the room, suck up all the air until she fainted for want of it. She tried to rub these cobwebby visions from her eyes, but they rewove themselves.

Unable to bear it, she descended again to the forbidden corridor. Twice upon a time, Bluebeard's first wife pulled the oaken door. There her husband stood, massive in the room.

"Wife, what do you ask of me?" he demanded.

She shook her head. She did not comprehend.

"What more do you ask of me? What task, what whim? What more can I do for you?"

"Cut the hedges higher?" she suggested. She felt in need of privacy.

"I cannot," he answered. "I can only cut them lower." And he withdrew his sword from his scabbard and sliced off his head. It rolled around the floor, the blue beard atangle, hollering, "Faithless Eve. Pandora. Cursed curiosity. Disobedience."

The head rolled at her feet. She dodged, crying. "What? What does this mean?" This must be how fairy-tale brides go mad. The head rolled and bumped her ankles, tripping her, hollering, "Knowledge does not become you, No-name. Slattern." Then the head bit her ankle and rolled through the door. She bent to rub the pain. A ring of tooth marks tattooed her ankle a delicate blue. When she straightened, the stablehand stood shirtless in the corner. The grin on his face looked overtightened, a bridle about to snap. He sidled slowly toward her, making clucking and soothing sounds. The haft of his whip protruded from his breeches. She backed up.

"No," she said.

"Yes," he said, circling, approaching, reapproaching.

Later, she sat on the stone floor trying to mend her dress with her hands. The stablehand was gone, but his words lingered in the room: you want this, yes, yes, you do. "No," she said and pressed her forehead against her knees. A seam in the air had been ripped wide. She felt time fraying, minutes and seconds wriggling free of the warp and weft, a thousand tiny threads, and she could not find the selvage edge. You want this, yes, no. Or was it yes?

The room forces itself on her. You want this. My husband's head and a horseman's lust? You want this. She was uncertain. Who is writing this for me? She could not even be certain about the provenance of her desire, what she wanted, what indeed she knew or thought or thought that she knew. Except this—she knew this, that she wanted to subvert the narrative, that she was tired of having words push her around, that this was how they did it (although she wasn't sure who they were): they pushed you around with words, moved you here and there, made you think this or that, but they told you nothing—the words, the "they."

When Bluebeard returned, as was his literary wont, his wife was still unmended and was slowly starving herself for meaning on the stone floor of the forbidden room. She heard her marauder clomping down the stairs and through the arched corridor.

When he saw her huddled on the floor (even though he could plainly see that she'd disobeyed him) he demanded the key ring because that was his plot trope. "The key ring," he thundered— the verb of choice for ogres and angry husbands.

She tossed it with docility because she was more of an attribute than a character, but even with the limits of her vision, she could see where this was going.

For a moment, just a flickering one, Bluebeard felt tenderness for this woman whom he was about to murder even though he was not supposed to feel affection. But she was fair and beautiful and good, and she looked meek and helpless sitting in her shredded gown, he thought, violating her point of view, which was one of her few privileges, so fair, so meek that it seemed a pity to kill her even though he would.

His bride raised her eyes and voice to him. "What is the affinity between love and hate?" she asked.

"They are one."

"And fear and rage?"

"The other one, and both define the other to create themselves, and both create the other to define themselves." He plucked his beard.

"You are wise," she said.

"I am weathered," he answered, "old and wise to your woman ways."

"What is to become of me?" she asked, rising, her dress unfurling a thousand clawed pennants from her torso.

"I am going to murder you."

"Why?"

"So that my second wife can open the door and discover you dead, and my third wife can discover the two of you dead, and the fourth and so on and so forth." He loved explaining the clarity of his reasoning so much that he failed to notice that his bride was donning seven-league boots.

"But why? Why murder me?"

"Because I am Bluebeard, a murderer. That is what murderers do. We murder—preferably helpless, innocent, and decent people—old philanthropists or newborn babes or fair young maidens like yourself," he expatiated, failing to notice the circularity of his argument and his bride's face transmogrifying into a gorgon's.

"Faulty premise," his snake-haired bride said. "You have tangled yourself in a mathematical gnarl. The seventh wife sees the previous six, the sixth, the previous five, the fourth, and so on and so forth.

But the first wife, old father weirdbeard, what does the first wife see in the forbidden room that activates the terror necessary to activate the tale?" The snakes in her hair hissed.

She felt the seam in the air reknitting.

"What?" Bluebeard said, then, "witch."

"Nearly," she said.

He looked up and turned to stone, his beard no longer blue but a lovely pale pink granite.

And his bride slid from the third person and her Medusa head and said to the stone-deaf man, "Why should you be the one who always gets to travel? I'm getting the Rumpelstiltskin out of this dreary palace."

As I, Bluebeard's first wife, readied to leave, the old key ring whirled into the air and walked on its brass legs out the door and up the stairs to I know not where. I left my statuesque husband in his stone cell, leaving him to unriddle the theme of an empty room. In my seven-league boots, I ascended to my chamber in a quarter-step and selected my favorite gown, a cerise velvet. I dressed and packed a few necessities in my trunk, some crown jewels, some marzipan, a tinderbox, a dagger, then summoned the stablehand to prepare my steed.

Yes, reader, I left him. I left him no seven wives and seven lives. I left him unturned pages where he forever is doomed to remain Bluebeard in once upon a time, Bluebeard the murderer unmurdering forever, pointless and pink in an empty room. I left him, but first I fired the stable boy. I gave the canaries and the maidservants the run of the place, and I made no exception. I did not forbid them the forbidden corridor and door, the forbidden room. Nothing was withheld. I threw open the windows, the doors, the jewelry caskets, the larder. Bounty was theirs. I was onward bound. But I cannot tell you where. The narrative had not found its destination.

But without my tale, I was neither good nor fair. I wore my ogress face but had no appetite for children. I was neither bad nor remarkably ugly. Ordinariness sat on my shoulders like a weather-eroded gargoyle, and I felt time fibrillate before me like an endlessly bifurcating path, every decision-to-be incising a wrinkle in my face. A princess without a husband is like a magician without gloves. I no longer fit. I pressed my boots to the tapestried floor of the long hall and left to live neither happily nor unhappily in an un-evered after. Such is the lot of unmurdered wives. A key. A door. A lock. And the next ending, and the next unending, unwritten, ever unturned.

This could be last summer repeating itself. We are here, Albion, Josh, and me, on Maudie's lawn. An interlude that could be entitled "Waiting for Zoe"—waiting, as we have waited every summer, for Zoe's always unannounced arrival.

Then the screen door slaps. The bushes rustle. I look up and see a spinning wheel disappear into the overgrown hardhack. A teacup whistles by, skimming off Joshua's head. Josh sighs. Maudie's thin voice rises from the shuttered cottage, "Albion, they're rearranging everything, everything. But those summer-caters can't fool me. I know they're stealing me blind. The jeezly old garbage-eating thieves are gettin' thicker'n spatters. Worth no more than gull's spit." Another teacup sails through the air just off Josh's port temple.

"Hey Mama," Josh says, "maybe I best be shuffling along."

I shake my head. "Don't be silly," I say. "Maudie's just confused."

Maudie's been confused for weeks. She thinks that summer people are stealing her furniture. She thinks that Josh is a summer person. Some days she thinks that the gulls are summer people, or the summer people are gulls, or that the one is somehow responsible for the other. On bad days she thinks that Josh is a gull. On very bad days, she throws things at the gulls, at Josh. Today is a very bad day.

"Confused," Josh echoes. He narrows his eyes, clenches his teeth like he always does before he starts talking about Life on the Inside, always capitalized in my imagination. "Have I ever told you about Life on the Inside?" Josh asks, without pausing for a

response. "There was some confused, some crazy cats on the
Inside." He wedges the words between his teeth. "Like Eduardo.
Did I ever tell you about Eduardo?"

He has, of course, but again Josh doesn't wait for, doesn't want,
an answer. "He talked like this," Josh says, without altering his
voice, his teeth still clamped. "Ice at the spine, this guy. Mean and
dotty. Used to pretend his mattress was his old lady. Do you know
what I'm telling you?"

I nod patiently, superfluously. I wonder if Albion will return
soon.

"Until he thought his mattress was doing him wrong. He cut
her with a knife he'd filed from a spoon handle, sliced the stuffing
right out of her ticking." Josh chuckles—low and soft. "Yeah, and
Eduardo wasn't half as gone a cat as that old mama in her gilded
cage there." Josh nods toward Maudie's cottage. "You know what
I'm telling you? Like she's twice as crazy as a man married to Sealy
Posturepedic. ¿Comprende? I remember like yesterday this time
old Eduardo leans over to me. 'Hey Josh,' he said, 'let's you and me
have a little schmooze. I think the missus is cheating on me . . .'"

Poor Josh. I let him rattle on, rattle his cage, rattle his tin cup
against old prison bars, his words clanking their chains like ghosts
at disbelievers. Ignored, invisible, they float away. Boo yourself,
and be damned. Josh will never break out of the big house. But
he's been a successful fugitive even so—eluding time and nature.
The missing twenty years don't hang in pouches under his eyes,
don't wrinkle his forehead, thin his hair. Clear, brown eyes.
Smooth skin. Thick, black hair. He looks thirty rather than fifty.
But perhaps he's eluded time too well, outrun it by standing still.
Legs spinning like Wile E. Coyote's, he digs himself into the road,
a rut twenty years old, while the road runner beeps along. "All reet
Daddy." Josh's zoot-suited slang. Sometimes I think that there's
nothing sadder than hipness twenty years out of date, middle age
without a mirror combing three hairs over a bald spot. Josh runs
like a watch without hands.

"Eduardo was connected. I mean connected. He knew people
on the outside. He knew people who knew people."

The legs of a Pembroke table poke through the puckerbrush.

"Mandy," the milkweed hisses and parts. Albion peers at me from the shadow of his cap. Age has not been as kind to Albion as it has to Josh. The days are marked in creases and wrinkles as definite as the days of a calendar. But the wear suits him as if his face were meant to be middle-aged. And the new white in his hair blends with his sun-bleached blond. "How's she holding up?" he asks.

I make a balancing gesture with my hand. "So-so," I stage whisper.

Albion shrugs, then hoists the table onto his shoulders. It bobs away above the tangle of milkweed, sumac, elderberry, and chokecherry, grown so high Albion swims through it as if under water, unnoticed, undetectable. A phantom ship leaves no wake.

"Listen to a little Ella," Josh says, "That'd smooth her right out, wash that care right out of her hair."

I smile. "Maudie hasn't been herself," I say. "She's been a little off since Adam died of Agent Orange." Adam Marsh didn't really die of Agent Orange, but he'd been complaining about it for weeks, said summer people were spraying the island with it. The ash trees turned orange first. Adam dismissed it as an early fall. Then the North Road turned orange. Adam dismissed it as ferrous soil. When the ocean turned orange, Adam explained it as the red tide. The pond? Acid rain. The sky? Dust from that Philippine volcano. But when his hands, his own hands, turned against him, when his very veins pumped orange, he could no longer dismiss it. He constructed a lectern out of lobster traps in front of Ernie's Island Market and rattled his pages at Ernie's customers as they ducked in for elbow macaroni or a can of baked beans. "You see? I can't even read my speech," he yelled. "They've painted over my words. It's a communist plot. The summer people have gaffled onto some Agent Orange, and they're spraying the island with it. The seas are boiling over with the culch. Orange steam hangs a pall on the sky. And 'fire was cast into the sea,'" Adam recited, "'And the third part of the sea became blood and the sun and the air were darkened by reason of the smoke.'"

Ernie wasn't too pleased. He thought that Adam was distracting customers and cutting into his profits, but Minister Muckle loved it, thinking that it would kindle a little fire and brimstone in a few pagan bean-eaters.

Although Ernie was a bit harsh, most of the islanders judged Adam Marsh kindly: "Adam's crazy. He's always been crazy. Whole fam-damily's crazy since Cappy Marsh married his first cousin, Amanda Chandler, and inbred the first two island families." Whereupon another islander would tolerantly remark, "We're all the sinning offspring of Adam and Eve," or "Isn't a man on this island who isn't a Maine-iac," so they could bustle home and heat up their beans for supper feeling Christian, tolerant, open-minded.

When the mainland doctor pronounced Adam DOA at Maine Medical, he put a stop to the bean-eaters' open-mindedness. Massive coronary. Adam had been staring at the world through a lens of his own blood for weeks. Most of the islanders murmured about Adam being a right-thinking fellow and a woodpile cousin, and a few other elegiac et ceteras, but one pagan islander remarked that he'd been looking at the island through rose-colored glasses. The one-liner circled the island as fast as full moon high tide and crested as the opening line of Minister Muckle's memorial sermon—the theme: spiritual optimism.

"Mandy?" Josh asks, lighting a carefully rolled joint, "Do you think Zoe will ever get here?" He sounds breathless as he asks this, holding the sweet smoke tight in his lungs.

"Josh, why do you still smoke that stuff?" I ask. "Isn't that what got you into trouble in the first place?" For a moment, a cold blade rests on my tongue. The metal taste of fear. Murder. Josh's eyes mirror me coolly—prison eyes, Eduardo's eyes. If looks could kill, and it is not just a figure of speech.

A brass candlestick zips past, zeroing in on the blue spruce. The stiletto edge of Josh's gaze dulls.

"You know Zoe," I say. "She may come; she may not."

A grandfather clock's face peeks from the blue spruce.

"I hope she comes," Josh says. The sentence goes up in a puff of blue smoke.

"Last summer when Zoe was here, the island felt like old times," Albion says emerging from behind the clock. He slumps into an Adirondack.

"Yeah Daddy, you called Bingo with that one." Josh's eyes turn dull as a mirror's silver back. He's conversing with himself, the past.

"It was like Grandmother was young again," Albion continues, "things to do, places to go, laughs."

"On the Inside there was a guard like Zoe—alive, you know what I'm saying? Flesh and blood among the zombies."

Like Timex, Josh keeps right on ticking.

Albion lolls in the Adirondack, squinting out at the bay, the middle distance. "Jesus, Josh, " he says without looking at him, "stub that thing out. It's un-American. Go pour yourself a beer." But Josh doesn't hear him. He fogs himself in—nostalgia and blue smoke. The grandfather clock gongs once. Albion closes his eyes against the sun.

We're an odd group.

Albion is not really Maudie's grandson but a second cousin by marriage or twice-removed, or both, but, however related, Maudie raised Albion from a wee accident. During World War II his English-born mother bunked with an American serviceman. They married a month before Albion's birth. But Albion's father was soon airborne again. Albion rarely saw him. Alison, Albion's mother, brought him to the United States after the war, located her husband's relatives, and moved in with Maudie. She eventually divorced Albion's father. But twenty years elapsed before the decree; Albion's father always seemed to be in midair. Albion stayed on the island even after Alison moved back to England.

Albion's origins embarrass him. He thinks of himself as being as American as mass production and the right to bear arms. He draws himself in bold black lines sometimes bordering on comic-book caricature, speaking in clichés, repeating himself. I envision his adages in balloons floating over his head: Real men don't eat quiche; Close enough for government work; Life's a hardship tour. Albion—the cartoon balloon man.

Albion earned a degree from U. Maine, Orono, in English literature, but he didn't know what to do with himself after graduation. He returned to the island, loved a series of women, hated a series of jobs, and wound up hating his job as ferryman, deckhand on the Island Fantasy, carrying luggage for retirees and collecting fares from tourists. "It's become an island of old people,"

Albion often complained, "old people and real estate developers." He sometimes joked about his job: "I'm Charon," he said. "I pole the forgetful to the forgotten." Nothing over Lethe to nothing. He named his dog Cerberus.

Between boats, Albion now takes care of Maudie and her cottage. But he owns his own place. My friend Zoe stayed at Albion's last summer. I tried to bring them together, but it didn't seem to take. I've been in love with Albion for twenty years. That, too, didn't take. It couldn't.

Joshua grew up in the Bronx. Sometimes he claims his father was a rabbi, sometimes a haberdasher. In any event, when his father died, Josh took over as patriarch of the family. He disciplined his younger brothers; he disciplined himself. They studied Torah, went to temple, until Josh developed an interest in, then an addiction to, jazz. He immersed himself in the life—the streets, the tunes, the reefer. Hard times. Hard time. Josh entirely missed the Second World War; he spent it Inside.

When he got out of prison, Josh tried to find his personal promised land. He turned his back on New York and made his way north to Portland. He claims that he used to sit on the mainland beach and gaze across to the island. One day, stoned, he tried to walk across at low tide.

Eventually he took the ferry over and met Albion on the boat. They became unlikely friends. For a while, Albion dated one of Josh's friends, a summer person from the mainland. But it didn't work out. Albion introduced Josh to Zoe last summer, and Josh fell in love with her. Hopeless.

When I first met Josh, he was toting a cassette player—blaring trumpets, progressive jazz—thirty-year-old progressive. "Man, nothing's caught up to this stuff," he said.

Josh likes the island. "It's peaceful here," he says, as if hearing my thoughts, "like being dead." Between puffs, he surveys the spot—tumbling stone walls, the work of frost heaves, the abandoned cannery by the shore, the rotting pilings. "This place gave up the ghost years ago," he says.

I nod. A gull lands on the lawn and pecks at a teacup shard.

Maudie hates New Yorkers. She hated Josh on sight and sound.

But, initially, she battled it out quietly. He did not exist for her. When she first met him, she closed the door on his extended hand. She spoke to Albion as if Josh were not there. She spoke through him. She apparently did not even hear the syncopated din of Josh's tapes. He wasn't there. But that was before Josh became a seagull.

A sugar bowl grazes Joshua's ear. But he barely reacts, brushing at it as if it were a dragonfly. "Yeah, Mama, copacetic." He lies back on the grass. "It's beautiful. Like the sun and moon stand still here."

Like Albion, Josh has run through a series of jobs: green grocer, waiter, florist. He's between jobs now—on vacation. He's been on vacation since Zoe visited last summer. I don't ask how he survives, but his pockets jingle, lined with more than lint and marijuana seeds. Dream peddler.

Josh stares at the sky. Albion, disturbed by the beeper clipped to his pocket, shakes himself from his snooze and slowly rolls up from the Adirondack. He stretches tall, taller than the grandfather clock. The muscles in his arm, knotted like hemp rope, wrap around the clock body. "Boat time," he says, "check on Maudie for me," and elopes into the brush with the clock.

I hear Maudie as soon as I open the door, but I cannot see her in the low-ceilinged darkness of the cottage. My hip bumps a dough box. Maudie's strong, bony fingers wrap around my wrist.

"Make them stop," she begs. "Please make them stop."

My blind hand reaches into the darkness and strokes her wiry hair.

"I know you think I'm just notional, but look: they're stealing my things, my life." She whines, "my very life."

I pat her hair.

"Adam's clock," she says, "the one his father carved, the one he built, is gone. And I can't find my table. It was my mother's kitchen table. The summer people are moving everything around. I don't know where I am."

"You're at home, Maudie," I soothe her, "at home."

"Alison?" she asks.

"No, it's Mandy." My eyes begin to adjust to the darkness. Brass winks at me. Adam's convex mirror over the fireplace. The inclinometer on the walnut paneling. I get my bearings.

"Mandy," she says. "Did you bring me that recipe?"

"Recipe?"

"Recipe," Maudie snaps, "the one you promised me for currant jam. You gave me the wrong amount of sugar. Ruint the batch just 'cause you're trying to keep it to yourself since the grange prize. I want the right amount of sugar."

"Maudie, you're thinking of my grandmother. It's me." I bring my face closer. "Mandy." Named after my grandmother who was named after her grandmother.

"It's just like you, Amanda, to keep that recipe to yourself. You wouldn't lend a dying friend a kind word."

I brush her hair, her face. On bad days Maudie rolls through time as if it were a film in reverse, recent memories withdraw like shadows into dark corridors, but the details of decades-old characters and routines shine in full light. Adam's doctor diagnosed it as Alzheimer's.

As I stroke Maudie's hair, I realize that, for me, Maudie and Adam are the island in the same way eelgrass and granite block, salt marsh and clam flat, beach heather and barnacles are the island. Now that Adam's dead, Maudie's the oldest islander. Many islanders remember the old days, but few still live the old ways. Between them, Maudie and Adam gardened and lobstered, sailed and quilted, seined and spliced, rushed and splinted, clammed and canned, an endless array of island arts, before arthritis crippled Maudie's fingers and Adam's heart failed him. Maudie is island, is as authentic as the sand on Marsh Point. And as I stare down the dimness of the room, I think, Maudie is as genuine as her antiques, as the furniture relayed to her by generations of family—now a stolen, scattered history with a price tag displayed discreetly in mainland storefronts.

Maudie's crying subsides. She tries to shove my hands away. "Who is that?" she asks. "Stop making over me." Her fingers clamp onto my shoulders. "Amanda?" she asks and shakes me.

"Yes, Maudie, it's Mandy."

"Stop fussing over me and get down to the shore and fetch me some seaweed to mulch the garden."

"Sure, Maudie, sure." Maudie hasn't kept a garden in ten years.

"Get along now," she says, "before we get a frost." She heads for the kitchen.

"Okay, Aunt Maudie." I wonder if I should follow her into the kitchen. Sometimes my diplomacy, my deference paralyzes me. Maudie used to tell me, nicety has a price. I bang outside to join Josh on the lawn.

Maudie isn't really my aunt, but we are related. I'm a Chandler, named Amanda for a long line of mothers. Maudie was a cousin to one of them. Whichever one, Albion is my cousin, distant or near, so I could not marry him; although Maudie says Chandlers have been marrying Brewers for so long now that they've inbred the craziness out of the family, so small it disappeared, or sometimes she says the madness is so deep in the blood it's in the island groundwater.

Actually, Albion never asked me to marry him. We dated, of course. By now Albion's dated every unmarried island woman, summer and year-round, between the ages of twenty and forty-four. And most of them have since married, divorced—or both—someone and somewhere off-island. But Albion hasn't married, and I haven't married. I suppose that the bean-eaters have taken our eventual marriage for granted for so long that the possibility is as inbred as the Chandlers and the Brewers and their craziness. But the possibility has been so inbred that it's dried up the gene pool. Albion will not propose, because he knows that I will say yes. Albion is looking for someone like Maudie—tall and tough as the twisted pine on the north shore, gritty as the clam flats—a hunting partner, a mechanic, a cook, someone passionate, island-born, but, unlike Maudie, educated and independently wealthy. The woman does not exist. This comforts Albion.

I will not test his comfort. I cannot touch him. Over the years I've developed what I privately call my theory of relativity. Avoidance is easier than rejection. Inaction is safer than action. Long ago, after both my parents were killed in a boating accident,

I realized that kinship leads to loneliness, relatedness to alien-ation. It is the inborn paradox of community. On an island you feel apart, remote from the world. You have community without privacy, intimacy without understanding, a confusion of relatives tangled in their histories. I love the island. I love the people here. But geographically and psychologically, I explore distances, seek higher ground. That was why I decided to move away, to spend only summers here.

I also moved away because work on the island is scarce. You can clam, lobster, cater to tourists, or marry someone who clams, lob-sters, or caters to tourists. I left the island to go to college, to grad-uate school, and, eventually, to teach at a prep school in Massachusetts. I met Zoe at Hawthorne Academy.

I didn't know what to make of her. She still stands enshrined in my memory like some large-breasted goddess of plenty, a pre-Raphaelite figure blocked out in light and color as bold as stained glass, yards of blonde hair cascading down her shoulders.

"Zoe Marino," she said as she advanced toward me. "The per-son's as odd as the name." Her handshake, firm and certain, took my gentle grip by surprise. "What's yours?" she asked.

"What?" I asked.

"Your name," Zoe said.

"Amanda." I stammered.

"We're a couple of live ones, eh?" she asked, poking me with her elbow. "A Greek name and a Latin. What were our parents up to?"

I wanted to tell her that I didn't know, that my parents were dead, that I could not ask them. But in that moment of introduc-tion, she confounded me with her easy familiarity. A sister, I thought, my older sister, although Zoe actually was four years my junior.

We shared classrooms, faculty gossip, curricula and coffee, and a sense that we were strangers among xenophobes. We passed hours discussing novels, poetry, and men—always men—or the lack of them, reliving Zoe's broken love affairs and lust for new ones. I noticed other department members cast disapproving looks at Zoe, but I noticed only with my peripheral vision. She'd become as essential to me, as elemental, as air and water. But her

elements were earth and fire. In the Yankee quietness of our aca-
demic courtyards and Greek revival buildings, in the ivied pro-
priety of New England, Zoe's laugh resounded too loudly, her
hands gestured too expansively, her feet landed too decisively, her
appetites wandered, all too unrestrained, after the forbidden fruit:
wine, men, joy.

Once she finally noticed it, Zoe hated the hypocrisy of
Hawthorne. "This place goes on like the rest of the world—only
behind closed doors," she said. She suspected all of the teachers of
being reverends. Most of them were, and they weren't ready for
Zoe's gospel of requited love, expressed desires, and dedicated
frivolity.

In the fall semester, she tried to shake up the decorum of faculty
meetings a bit by bringing a jug of wine and loaf of bread into the
English office. "What's happening?" she asked, thumping the jug
down on the department head's desk. In the embarrassed silence, I
wanted to be her guide through New England. I wanted to lead her
through the rings Yankees draw around themselves. I wanted to
explain the history to her—the sense that whatever is happening
has happened already, that New England's living, breathing self lies
at the center of those rings, circumscribed by history. But I could
not explain this to her. She understood it, but she did not accept it.
"History is process, progress," she said. "Not here," I said. Our
colleagues politely declined a glass of Gallo. We bravely shared a
paper cup.

My alienation at Hawthorne was my alienation anywhere:
Yankee solipsism, the result of too many, too long winters. But I
found a home in our improbable friendship. I loved Zoe all the
more because I knew that her presence was ephemeral. She would
return to the Midwest. I pictured her there, thrashing around in
endless fields, dynamic, productive like an anthropomorphized
threshing machine. John Deere. Her sense of adventure, of possibility, excited me. Like the blonde perched on the back of a red
convertible, she waved at the parade of spectators. Once, in our
pillow talk, I confessed this image, Zoe as reigning celebrity. She
laughed in my face, that loud unabashed laugh. "Amanda," she
said, "you're always symbologizing. Life shouldn't mean but be."

"You don't mean that," I said.

And she laughed louder.

A year ago we sat on this lawn—Zoe, Josh, and me. Adam was alive, and Maudie had fewer bad days. I lean over and pick up a teacup shard. I sense Josh studying me, and glance up at him. The smoke wisps in front of his face in long, spectral bars. "You okay, Mama?" he asks.

"I'm fine, Josh. I was just thinking about Zoe."

"Yeah." Josh nods. "I can dig. We broke bread together a few times. You know what I mean; we sat down to table, friends for life." He sighs. "On the Inside I sat down with some mean dogs, mad dogs. You had to cover your plate, man. You know what I'm telling you."

My turn to sigh. While Josh rambles, I play an old game. Squinting to reverse time, I imagine the leaves off the trees, the green from the grass, the sun from the sky. The world turns white in a great, obliterating blizzard. In the winter, I ignore the frozen ground, imagine the sun filling the sky, coaxing the buds into leaf. Sometimes I focus on the power plant across the bay and imagine it away. When CMP built the plant ten years ago, Maudie took it as a personal affront. "They spoilt the view," she said.

For the first few years, she insisted that she could hear the underwater cables humming. She complained that it kept her awake nights. She predicted that it would electrocute all the mackerel, the harbor seals. But she no longer mentions the plant, inhabiting a time before it was built, occasionally even a time before electricity came to the island.

Josh homes in on the nearer past. "We sat here, yeah, dipping into a little salmon, a little Soave, some cheese. I think we slept together the night before. Yeah, because Albion was uncomfortable—like there'd been this undefined thing going on with him and Zoe, remember?"

"I remember," I say. "Zoe was staying at Albion's, clearing brush around the place for him for room and board."

Josh laughs. "Yeah, she was one tough mama with that scythe."

I laugh, too, seeing her again, her blonde hair braided, her forehead, wet, hacking away at the underbrush. "The things I do for love," she said. That night Albion threw a clambake. After many hours and bottles of wine, Zoe and Josh wandered off, smoked some dope, and made love on the beach. All along, Zoe and I had thought she'd wind up with Albion. Accidental regrouping. I was left alone with Albion at the fire. It was quiet after Zoe left. The air moved slowly, sadly. Albion leaned over me, wrapped his arms around me in an embrace seven years old, as familiar as when we were lovers. I felt the old, old craziness, the passion. But the kiss ended abruptly. Albion turned his face from me. "Loose lips sink ships," he said. I wanted to swear at him, kick him. But we're family. It's a small island.

"Yeah, she stayed at Albion's," Josh says, "but she never stayed with him. But we got it together the night of the clambake. Things were really happening for us. It could be for us, you know. I could be nice to her, nice. Yeah, there was something there. Special."

I nod, although I remember differently. In the morning Zoe sat in the Adirondack telling me what I already knew: she wasn't returning to Hawthorne at the end of the summer. She wanted to do something with computers, word processors, write software manuals perhaps. She might move to California. Joshua sat on the grass at her feet, trying to interrupt, to tell her that he loved her. She waved him off with a paperback copy of *The Great Gatsby* as if he were a logy bee. Josh passed her the bottle of Soave. She drank some. He passed her some Havarti. She ate some. But their night was over. I felt sorry for Josh.

"Zoe's special," I say. I look across to the pier and see the ferry tied up to the float.

"Yeah, so, maybe we'll get it together again when she comes out this summer. We could pick up where we left off. We wouldn't waste so much time this time 'round, you know. 'Cause she worked through that thing with Albion. Like, he's too cold for her, too far away. Cold to her hot." Josh stops suddenly. Albion stands by the spruce. His face distorts with some emotion that I do not recognize. I wonder how long he's been standing there. In the moment before he speaks, time elongates, stretches so thin that it disappears. Timelessness.

Then Albion speaks. "Zoe stayed with me, Josh," he says. "With me," he repeats, then strides off toward the cottage.

I squeeze my eyes shut, trying to block out the power plant, but the game fails. Albion and Zoe. The sun cuts my eyelids. Sharp heat. Light shatters. Albion and Zoe. I imagine water, winter. I try to cool my face.

Josh says, "You know, I don't think Zoe's coming this summer. Sometimes I don't think she's ever coming back."

"Didn't you hear him, Josh?" I ask. "Albion and Zoe. Did you know that?"

Josh doesn't look at me, doesn't answer me.

"Why didn't anyone tell me?" I ask.

Josh stares at me blankly. "What?" he asks.

"Doesn't anything register with you?" I ask. I am crying.

Josh peers at the spruce where Albion stood a minute ago. "We need some tunes," he says. He picks a teacup handle from the grass and scrutinizes it, puzzling out some mystery. A stoned archaeologist with a bone china clue on which an entire civilization depends.

"Josh, did you know?" I ask him. My voice sounds like a slap. I see the chill drop into his eyes again. He peers at me meanly from behind it.

"I know what I know," he says. "And some things you know, you're better off not knowing."

"Cut the cryptic prison shtick. Did you know?"

But Josh hides behind his eyes, lights up another joint.

Last summer's nights blur together—Zoe and me gossiping over a bottle of wine. "There's potential there for you and Albion," I said over and over. "It will never happen," she told me. "Albion's too private, too careful." Her disappointment reassured me. She must have known it. She must have known everything. She slept on Albion's couch, she told me, never getting more intimate than morning coffee. Albion composted the grounds. Our gossip gave me a glimpse of his private life, his bachelor habits. Zoe and I laughed about his quirks, and all that time another laughter, too high-pitched for me to hear, rose above our own: Zoe and Albion's collusive chuckling at my ignorant hope, my vicarious dreaming, indecent dreaming. My skin burns.

Albion and me. Zoe and me. Zoe and Josh. Zoe and Albion. The shifting configurations dizzy me. Did I ever really want Albion and Zoe together, or did I hope for it only because I thought it impossible? And what difference does it make; does it finally make any difference at all?

"Don't wish too hard for your heart's desire," Maudie used to say. "You just might get it."

A teacup strikes my temple. "Wake up," Josh yells. Our eyes lock in surprise. His hand catches itself, stops. Before I can think what to say, Albion stands before me. "Where the hell is Maudie?" he asks. "I asked you to keep an eye on her."

"In the garden," I say, looking away from him, squinting him out of the picture.

Albion's hands reach for me, shake me. I stare at the creases at the corners of his eyes, such cool blue eyes, recalling the last time that I was this close to him, his eyes.

"What garden?" he asks. "What were you thinking of?"

My eyes close, and he is gone. The power plant disappears. Josh goes up in smoke. And Zoe is plowed under, corn cobs and husks plowed deep into dark, secret soil. The air dies on my skin.

When I open my eyes, Albion stands on the lawn, an arm around Maudie's waist. Josh's face presses into the grass. Maudie's sobbing. "They've taken my garden. I planted snow peas this year, and they're gone. Every one." A trowel dangles meaninglessly from her hand. "And my corn. It was just beginning to tassel."

Albion leans over her, comforting. "It's all right, Maudie. It's all right. It's a hardship tour, but you're going to be okay."

"Where's Adam?" Maudie asks, and she stares unseeingly at me. "Where have they taken Adam?"

"Adam's dead," Albion says, "and the garden's fallow. It's been unplanted for years."

"My table," Maudie pleads, "my clock."

"I've been taking them," Albion says. "I had to sell them, Maudie, to pay the taxes."

"You?" Maudie asks, "Albion?" She pushes Albion's arm from her waist and turns toward the shore. Hands on her hips, Maudie silently confronts the bay, the power plant looming over it. Deliberately, carefully, she turns and walks toward Josh. No one moves as the neat toe of her black shoe kicks his ribs. No one moves as Maudie says, says very softly, "You, Joshua, I want you out of here. I want you and your drugs off my property, back where you came from."

Joshua uncoils, curls up. His torso twists. His wrists snap apart, unshackle as if he were breaking links of air. "Get out of my face," he hisses. His hand flattens, his palm arcs through the still air, an inevitable momentum of skin to skin.

Maudie's arms clench against her chest. The world see-saws. Maudie's lying on the ground. Joshua stares at the red palm of his right hand as if it were speaking earnestly, urgently but in some foreign tongue. And Albion's dashing for the cottage. Maudie's eyes roll up toward the sky—green as sea water, resigned as a jigged mackerel's. Then Albion's kneeling over her, breathing into her, the heels of his hands pumping her chest. The beeper on his pocket punctures the air. The rescue van rips up the road. Dust and snapping branches. Machines. A stretcher. Maudie and Albion swirl away. Sirens and lights.

I sit, these scenes flickering before me. I watch Josh stuff his matches, a pipe, and a Baggie into his pocket, pick up his tapes and cassette player. I watch his mouth open and close for the words that do not come. I watch him walk to the beach, pick his way through the driftwood until the curve of the cove swallows him up.

The color drains from the day. Still I sit, posed in the dark like an empty glass, a still life waiting for a paintbrush to fill me with color.

The ferry crosses. A raccoon thrashes into the spruce. Children's voices drop into the rocks along the beach. The ferry crosses, its port and starboard lights, pinholes in the fabric of the night. Albion finds me in the dark.

"She's going to make it," he says.

I nod. "And Joshua," I ask, "did you see Josh?"

Albion pauses, considering how to answer this, then says, "I'd better not see him. I don't want to see him around here."

I want to tell Albion that Josh didn't mean it. I want to say that he was stoned, tangled up in time, prison ethics. But instead I say, "Out on the last rail before sundown? This island ain't big enough for the both of you?" My voice as dry as sand.

Albion says, "He made his bed; now he can lie in it." And I see the words float in a blurb over his head, then sail away like a helium balloon, free on the Fourth of July.

"And Zoe," I ask, "what about Zoe?"

Albion says simply, "I loved her, Mandy. Something happened. Things happen fast with Zoe. And then it stopped, and she left." His hands wave as if they were searching for something to do, something to hold, a rope to cleat.

"Why didn't you tell me?" I ask. "Why didn't you tell me the truth?" But the questions have no urgency now. And I stare at my own hands, willing them to keep still.

Albion chuckles. I feel the cottage behind us, Maudie's ghost of a garden, Adam's pile of lobster traps. After a while, Albion asks, incredulous, "Tell you? Mandy, no one can tell you anything. You made up your mind about everything years ago. You were born with your mind made up, the whole picture arranged. What possible difference could it have made?"

And this, I know, is the truth, a truth like Zoe's not coming back to the island. The truth bears down on me like the power plant crouching somewhere on the dark horizon—an unseen but incontrovertible presence. I feel Zoe dwindling into a series of postcards, less and less frequent, the transcription of generic lies: Wish you were here; missing you; the years sure fly by. The truth has set her free. And for me—the truth that the truth doesn't change changes nothing. The truth changes nothing.

"I'm glad Maudie's going to be okay," I say, and when Albion doesn't answer, I say, "She's the last native."

Albion shakes his head. "Mandy," he says my name sadly. "Maudie wasn't . . . isn't," he corrects himself, "a native. She was born off-island, in Boston. She didn't move to the island until she was ten."

"But she's a Chandler," I say.

"A Boston Chandler, a whole different branch of the family tree."

"But it's the same family."

"The whole island's the same family," Albion says. "We're family," he adds. He leans over me and kisses my cheek, kindly, dismissively, and rustles off into the shadowy brush.

I, like Josh, like Maudie, am lost in the maze of my past, and I am no longer certain what was real, is real. There is only this: a patch of ground beneath my feet, this ground, this island. What could Zoe, always moving, know of islands? It takes time to develop history. Time in place. I envy Zoe her mobility. She gets away. She keeps escaping. I have only this: the island.

The fog rolls in overnight. The sun lurks behind it, trying to slice through the fog, demarcating the line between night and day, but the line blurs. I wake up to the fog and yesterday's losses: Maudie, Zoe, and Josh are gone. In some sense, Albion, too. And nothing is changed. I dress in the moist darkness.

As I walk through the mist to the shore, I remember one of the first things Josh ever told me. He was stoned; he said that he felt as if the island had slipped its mooring and was drifting away, nudging toward the edge of the earth. All these drifting continents going bump in the night. "I think Josh has slipped his mooring," Zoe said later in the kitchen. And we laughed. But Josh was right.

I reach the back shore where year after year the tide deposits another layer of silt and mud and debris, mouthfuls of land chomped off on the ocean side and washed up here. The fog is so thick that I cannot see the ferry, but I hear the foghorns moan— warning other boats of their proximity.

Before Brewers and Chandlers, the Indians landed here to hunt the foxes who hunted the rabbits before the Indians came. And what, I wonder, greeted the Indians here when discovery still seemed possible, and the sea stretched outward as limitless as imagination. Sun, rock, salt, and the meaningless cycle of days. What mattered here before history assigned a meaning to time, place, event? Sun, rock, salt, and the meaningless cycle of days.

The water drains from the flats, stranding crabs and minnows in the pools. The fog withdraws slightly, edging toward the hook. At the water's edge, taking form magically from the mist, a blue heron stands on one leg, perfectly still, his fine neck arched like the whorls of fog curling around him. His world becomes him. Then his wings reach and dissolve back into fog. My eyes search for him as if their vision depended on seeing him just once more, as if the sight of a blue heron in the mist might alter this world. Disappointed, they turn toward the shore. And I walk slowly back to the house.

We Who Live Apart

EDNA

The first childless woman I ever knew fried doughnuts in Taylorsville, Vermont, where I lived as a child. Edna Bone's small gray cottage overlooked the lake just below our house on the dirt road, and, on Saturday mornings, my father would send me with a sweaty quarter down to Edna's for crullers. I'd approach the Dutch door and rap on the bottom half until Miss Bone cracked the top and peered at me, her eyes deep but clear in the rugged terrain of her face. "What do you want?" she'd yell.

"A half dozen crullers," I'd whisper.

"What do you want?" she'd yell again, more loudly.

"A half dozen crullers," I'd mumble to my feet. Miss Bone was deaf, a condition I mistook for anger. But somehow she eventually understood and handed me a paper sack already blotting with grease.

While Edna counted out the doughnuts into the sack, I'd stare at the apples tacked up on strings all along the eaves of her cottage. Some bobbed, freshly peeled and firm, in the breezes that blew off the lake. Others, older, had already shriveled into character. Cheeks emerging. A nose protruding. Brows scowling into the features that would determine their personalities. And the most wizened ones, already tinted with paint, blue eyes, rouged mouths, haunted weirdly about the corners of the house, bald and bodiless like babies waiting to be born, or old men begging for the grave. In addition to doughnuts, Edna Bone made apple-head dolls.

Inside the Dutch door, on rows of shelves, farmers bent creased faces over their rakes, grandmothers knitted, children flew kites, a high-cheeked mother rocked a tiny cradle. Then Edna would block out the shelves of dolls, thrust her face and the paper sack forward and ripple her wrinkles into what I suppose now was a smile, which sent me bumping and terrified back up the road to our house.

Edna died sometime after the town tarred the road. And the new summer people who bought the adjoining land tore down the gray cottage. Because Edna had no children.

MY FAMILY

My brother: my brother Gary was six years younger than I. When I first told Gary that I was going to marry Wade Mills, we were walking along the road by Christian Hill. I spotted some daffodils—it was early spring after a hard winter—nodding over the brook, rushing with the meltwater, that runs dry in summer. "Let's pick them," I said and gamboled down the bank, snapping the daffodils off by the handfuls. Gary said he thought that we'd better not, but he did anyway, and it made it all the more exciting to pluck as many as we could before the rector roared out of the church hall and chased us up the bank. We sprinted, spilling daffodils and laughter, running with our arms full all the way home. We put the flowers in water on the kitchen windowsill. While we recovered our breath, we drank lemonade. Gary clinked the ice cubes in his glass and said how it was too bad that daffodils went by so fast. He sipped some lemonade, then said that he did not want me to marry Wade, because married people always moved away. I do not remember how I responded.

Years later, when my divorce came through, my brother sent me daffodils, bulbs and all. He's married now and lives in Ohio. We don't see much of each other. He has children.

My mother: when I was very sick, my mother would let me crawl into great-grandmother's canopy bed in the master bedroom, and she would drape the sides with quilts, so that I could huddle privately with my illness inside the makeshift tent. She'd bring me milk-tea and common crackers when I wasn't sleeping.

And, in the afternoons, she'd set her jewelry box on the side of the bed, and we'd poke through her pins and necklaces, coins and rings. I'd pull out an amethyst dripping six freshwater pearls and say, "This is beautiful. . . . And where'd you get *this* one?" And she'd smile, because, by the time I was six, I knew every piece and its origin, and she'd say, "That was grandmother Sawyer's baby ring." And, after we'd emptied the jewelry box onto the spread and sorted the rings and bracelets, occasional photos or safety pins into piles, we'd tuck them all back into their velvet compartments, and my mother would tuck me back into my tent and sit on the edge of the bed until I fell off to sleep. When my mother died, she left me her jewelry box.

My father: my father loved to joke although I never knew him to hurt anyone when he was about it—except once. After they put my grandfather in the ground and the priest clicked hurriedly through the rosary because the sky threatened snow, we all went to Aunt Esther's house. My father drank his preference, whiskey, and more of it than was usual. Aunt Esther pulled out Grampa's scrapbook and asked, "Remember when Dad bought that old Dodge?" and "Remember when Dad won first prize for his carnations?" My Dad just glanced down over Esther's bulk—Esther was what we called big-boned—and said, "Jasus Esther, this is deadly. Let's put a little spirit into this party." He fumbled a Glenn Miller album onto the Victrola and hoisted my mother up to dance. They fox-trotted while Gary and I sat on the floor and made faces at each other until we couldn't stop laughing. Gary had this killer face where he popped his eyes out and pursed his lips like a carp, all bulge-eyed. We felt lighter then until my mother suggested my father dance with Esther. My father shook his head mock-sadly. "I would if I could get my arms round both of her," he said. And we laughed. Even Esther. But my father couldn't stop there, and he cracked joke after joke about Esther's heft with tears streaming down his laugh crinkles and choking his laughter until my mother told him to knock it off. My father glanced at Esther who looked smaller all of a sudden, thinner than Dad's jokes. He sobered instantly, turned to me and asked, "Katie, do you want to go for a ride?" And we walked outside into the solemn darkness and climbed into the front seat of the old Ford wagon, but Dad never started the car. We sat, and, by the light sifting over the lawn from the living room window, I could see my father crying, and I could not say a word because I'd never seen him cry before.

At last he wiped his face with the rough back of his hand, unembarrassed, and he said, "I was never close to my father. But I can tell you this, Katie, I knew him. I knew him better than anyone in the damned family. I knew him better than anyone."

Esther died the year after my father and left Grampa's scrapbook to me. Because she never had children.

I never decided not to have children; time simply decided for me. One day I realized that not only did I not have any children, but also that I never was going to have any children. I turned thirty that year, and, shortly after my birthday, Wade and I split up. We were rather unremarkably unhappy. And we were no happier and no sadder apart than together. We separated as easily as a perforated certificate of marriage. I moved to Barre to teach high school English, where I still teach. Wade remarried and moved somewhere in New Hampshire. I do not know if he has children.

I found my dog after two years of teaching. Driving home to my apartment after a faculty meeting, I spotted a black and white puppy trotting into the circle of rain whirling in my headlights. I pulled onto the shoulder, put her in my car, brought her home, and fed her some torn bread and bacon grease in a chipped saucer. I tried to locate the owner, but no one ever claimed her, and I've had her ever since, twelve years.

My dog: people who have children but no dogs, or children and dogs, do not understand people who have dogs but no children. I suppose they think dog owners eccentric. But I do not throw my dog birthday parties, and I do not dress her in sweaters. People who do not have children simply need something that will rise like water to fill the volume of their lives. I, like other childless people, need a presence to shed hair into the dustless, quiet corners of my days, something to color in the blankness outlined by the definite, black contours of family. My dog does this.

I named my dog Sam Walter Foss for a poem by him entitled, "The House by the Side of the Road." But I call her Fossie, because she is a girl even if she is a spay. The poem reminds me of how I found her, and the first stanza reads:

> *There are hermit souls that live withdrawn*
> *In the peace of their self-content;*
> *There are souls, like stars, that dwell apart,*
> *In a fellowless firmament;*
> *There are pioneer souls that blaze their paths*
> *Where highways never ran—*
> *But let me live by the side of the road*
> *And be a friend to man.*

I keep the poem tacked up on my classroom door at school. Some of the younger teachers point out that it actually is a weak poem. But, weak or strong, it is how Fossie got her name.

I suppose sometimes I do seem eccentric to people who have children. When I am home, I talk to Fossie. Not that I expect her to understand or answer, but, even so, an implicit communication evolves between a dog and a woman who has no children. Fossie intuits which words apply to her and which are my own mumblings about recipes or lesson plans, perhaps by my inflection. And I understand her movements, anticipate her desire to be fed or let outside. It is less communication, perhaps, than a complicity of temperament and shifting moods. The words I speak to Fossie mean nothing. A relationship between a dog and a childless woman is an ineffable one, fostered by years of habit.

Still, although I understand all this, there are moments when I would be embarrassed to have a person present with us. I inherited a small summer cottage my parents kept on an island in Maine, and, in the summer, Fossie and I drive up to open the house and spend days of salt and sun. When we cross the long bridge that spans the border between New Hampshire and Maine, I wake Fossie up, beep the horn and whoop and try to stir her enough to poke her nose out the window, breathe the salt scent and silty clam flat smell. My parents similarly woke us up as children, and to cross the border without hooting and hollering would make me feel as if we were driving on aimlessly. Without the border clamor, the grand state of Maine would cease to be a state for me altogether.

WHAT I DO IN MAINE

When you are on vacation and do not have children, you have less to do and more time to do it in. I garden some, but, although I love flowers, I really do not like to garden. I guess that I expect plants to grow of their own volition. No coaxing. I don't mind scattering a packet of seeds and covering them with a thin crumble of soil, but then I expect the shoots to fend for themselves. I weed a little, but I don't fertilize the ground or thin young plants. Those that make it, do; those that don't, don't. Still, the garden thrives. I plant only perennials. Bleeding hearts, sweet William, and baby's breath come up, thick as a mat, year after year, surviving my puttering and negligence.

When it rains, I read or piece a quilt, although we've more quilts than beds, because my mother and grandmother before me also stitched away the tedium of rainy days. But I like watching the patterns taking form and, square by square, checker out a quilt.

I visit with the neighbors, of course, about the weather, or the effect of all that rain on rosebushes, and tsk-tsk over island illnesses and deaths and whatever teenager is drinking beer this year down in the cove. Sometimes we talk about my parents or the occasional postcard from my brother.

They are quiet summers, but I like them. On the fairest days when the wind flaps the clouds around like clean laundry, Fossie and I walk down to the sand beach. Fossie sprawls on the beach and squirms on her back to scratch it. And I look out over the limitless stretch of sea to where it vanishes in a haze, and sea and sky blur—indistinguishable.

The surf is gentle at the beach. The sun is hot. From somewhere down the way drift the voices of children. Always the same voices, though the children change. My voice once, the voice that drains away with the last hint of pink from the sky. And I listen to the waves suck at the sand and drag it out and out, baring shells, gnarled fists of seaweed, and bleached wood like old bones on the drying shingles. And when Fossie draws up near me and lies panting on the sand, I note how she is aging, shriveling into being, her skin tightening, fur burrowing deeper into her eye sockets. And I know that she doesn't understand me when I toss a mussel shell at the hard band of wet sand and watch it drop short of the water and say, "Memory can be an awful thing."

The Bowlville Cemetery

Luther Shedd had had it. All his life, he'd been cold, and all his death—so far. Simply put, he didn't like being underground. And for one reason: he hated being cold, so much so that he had demanded in his Last Will and Testament that his epitaph read, "I Told You I Was Cold." For another, he was riled that no one prepared a body for the experience of interment.

Sure, Luther had known for years that he'd be buried in the family plot, but no one had forewarned him that he'd be conscious. No one had ever mentioned that decay would be a sensate experience, that lying horizontally just below the frostline in a dark box the size of a closet with nothing warmer on than your Sunday suit would be a mite uncomfortable. But Luther Shedd was in a position to verify that it was very uncomfortable indeed. And he had had enough. So he got up.

Truth to tell, Luther had never been a patient man—in life as in death. He was impatient, in point of fact, impatient and even abrupt, cranky and even cantankerous, and some would have said downright dump-dog mean. To clarify, at the time of Luther's death, not one soul in Bowlville expressed anything except relief, and occasionally skirls of giddy delight.

The minister made his rounds, trying to find someone to say a word for Luther at the service. Caleb, the store owner, said, "Wouldn't you know that cheap old curmudgeon—sorry, Reverend—would leave without settling his tab."

His neighbor, Miss DeJardin, who rarely spoke above a whisper, clapped her thigh and exclaimed, "I'm glad that he finally hauled his sorry posterior—sorry, Reverend—off this mortal coil."

Alden, Luther's hired man of many years before he opened his repair shop, said only, "Whee."

Luther's daughter, Carol Jean, remarked his passing by observing, "There is a God." She declined to speak for her father at the service, but she did offer Minister Howe a doughnut.

Minister Howe finally spoke for the town himself. The elegy was terse but trenchant. "Luther Shedd came and went. People 'round here noted him for his particularly clean and well-mended shirts." Of course, Carol Jean washed and mended her father's shirts—usually following a beating—but this passed without comment as Minister Howe had found something nice to say. But it had taken some effort on his part.

Luther Shedd had been the sort who would go out of his way to be unpleasant. He'd cross a road to tell Mrs. Goodall, "Jeezum, that kid of yours gets homelier by the minute." If someone brought a pie by at Christmas, he'd point out that the crust had been better the year before last. He drank. He cheated at cards, business, pleasure, and every possible turn. He was stingy. He beat his wife until she ran away in the middle of the night and drowned trying to ice-walk the river. The town didn't find her body until ice-out in spring, blue and beautiful in a snaggled cove below the spillway. Luther didn't attend the funeral. He was busy selling his wife's old clothes to a rag dealer.

But Luther had just enough mean sense not be inspired about it. He never crossed the line, teetered on the edge of the diabolical. There was no genius about him, no demonic theater. No, Luther was too mean for that. That might inspire awe or, at very least, diversion. Luther had no desire to entertain anyone. He was perfectly mean.

It is a singularity of meanness that it elicits the accommodation of others. No one knows quite how to deal with it, so people tend to tiptoe around it, feeling (perversely) ashamed. Luther could interrupt a town meeting just to yell, "Criminately, Lester Coleburn's so fat that I can't bear to look at him." Or he'd tromp into the store and say, "Only a Christly fool would buy this overpriced stale crap they stock here." And Selectman Coleburn would blush and check his coat buttons and no one would come to his defense or contradict Luther. And whatever fool was buying a loaf of moldy bread would lower his eyes and bang out the door, forgetting his change. True, Coleburn was fat and the stock was steep and stale. But Luther's reminding everybody only compounded the shortcomings. Luther had a way of making people feel that life itself was shameful, and so were their small roles in it. Where Luther stood, meanness ruled. No one ever spoke up against Luther—except once.

Luther once commented to Caleb's teenage son, Gary, the older boy, "Jeezum Crow, your face has more pimples on it than my buttocks."

Gary jutted his chin, readying an "oh yeah?" look. He stammered a bit as he said, "It has less hair, too."

Luther rubbed his grizzled chin. "I expect. Most Nancy-boys don't got no face hair."

Gary tried to recover his stride. He may have been trying to say something about Luther being the only ass he'd ever seen with a beard, but the tension got to him. His mouth just went woolly on him and his lips squirmed, and he said, "Yeah. Yeah. Na. SMA-meer splut, splut." Then he stared at his chest where he'd spattered spit all over his shirt.

Luther guffawed. He had a mean laugh. But people respect meanness. Some others in the store joined in. For a year after, every time Luther saw Gary he said, "Yeah. Yeah. Na. SMA-meer splut, splut." He even had a mean memory.

It's odd that niceness doesn't have the same effect. People don't feel any need to accommodate it or join in. If you walk up to Miss DeJardin and say, "Pretty hat," she'll just say, "Thank you," or demur, "This old thing?" If you walk up to some mother and say, "What a beautiful baby," she pretty much takes it in stride.

Nice is nice. Mean is powerful. Luther's daughter was nice, and he decided to go to see her first. There were sightings, of course, on the way.

A corpse cannot just take a notion to sit up in its coffin, scrabble out of its grave, lurch, tattered and rattling, down the streets, clumping clods of dirt as it heaves home without people taking notice—especially when that corpse was a person universally disliked when living—as Luther was. So the word was on the street that Luther—or some stinky cadaver that resembled him—was out and about. "Damn," people said. "Wouldn't you know it. He was too mean to live and too mean to die."

Luther didn't knock at the door. It had been his home, so he felt a sense of entitlement. He staggered in and collapsed in the captain's chair beside the woodstove and commanded, "Build a fire. I'm cold."

Carol Jean stared at her father's remains. "You would come back, wouldn't you? Just out of pure spite."

Luther demanded again, "Build a fire. I'm cold," this time rattling and rapping his finger bones on the tabletop.

But Carol Jean did not respond. It wasn't that Luther had lost his meanness; he was just as mean as ever. Nor had he lost any power. What he had lost was his voice. When Luther thundered, Carol Jean only heard the clatter of his jawbone and the teeth that remained him, the rattle and click of his bones like some hackneyed haunter from a fireside tale.

It took Luther a while to realize that he had lost his impact. He was cold, but, voiceless, he commanded no authority. He tried spooking her with a bogeyman glare and a gangly skeleton jig and a hair-raising jaw clack, but Carol Jean just said, "Knock it off, you old ham. You're raising dust." He knocked it off; his heart wasn't in it anyway. He did rise, however, and wrap himself in an afghan while Carol Jean turned back to her deep-frying. Afghan aflutter, Luther pegged out the side door to catch some afternoon sun.

Normally when a dead person returns to town, you might expect a little small talk, a little curiosity. "Hey, what's it like on the other side?" "Did you see Aunt Margaret?" "What's up with the white light?" Or at least, "Long time, no see. What you been up to?" But Luther Shedd's return prompted no such neighborly inquiries. People had been happy to see him go, and they were not pleased to see him return.

Going underground had not altered Luther much. He was thinner and bonier but just as mean as ever. Just as mean and twice as bored. His boredom soon had him haunting the general store, where he'd trip people going in and out or sit in the sun and remove his jawbone and terrify the children or glare with his eyeless sockets at Calista DeJardin, who was shy and walked with downcast eyes at the best of times, and these were not the best of times.

People started saying that something must be done, but nobody said what. Minister Howe opined that Luther had returned to redeem his life, but no one was buying that interpretation. As Caleb said, "Luther Shedd is mean to the bone." People generally agreed—Luther Shedd: Unwanted, Dead or Alive. But no one knew how to get the old reprobate back underground.

The Bowlville Cemetery Committee called an emergency meeting. The members agreed that they were overtaxed to find a solution, their usual business being lawn care, dog-shooing, plot sales, and coping with the occasional Halloween prank. It was one-armed John, who scythed the cemetery hardhack, who suggested that the committee approach Augustus Mason, the undertaker.

One-armed John represented the committee.

In his dusky parlor, Augustus heard John out. "I'm sympathetic," he said, "but what do you want me to do about it?"

With a deft motion, John stuffed his pipe with his thumb, struck a match on the base of the bowl, and pulled a long draw. Through a screen of smoke, he said, "You're the undertaker. Undertake him."

"Criminy, John. It's not like being a dogcatcher. This is outside my line of work. You need a specialist."

John nodded and wordlessly departed, his left sleeve dangling like a plaid ghost. He was stymied.

Carol Jean was having the hardest time of it, with Luther huddled in her kitchen, clicking and clacking his grinning mandible at her. It put her on edge. And the smell. The old man was whiffy. Rackety-clack and phew. It was getting old. And he was up to his usual nastiness, too, switching the salt and sugar so she spoiled a batch of doughnuts, tossing a fresh wedge of cheese into the fryer. Just plain mean. But after a nerve-wracking week of Luther's clapping jaw and tackety teeth, she finally figured out that he was trying to tell her something, so she fetched a tablet and pencil, and said, "What?"

With his bony digits, Luther painstakingly scrawled a spidery "I'm cold."

"Shoot," Carol Jean said. "That's yesterday's fish." And she went back to her doughnuts.

But Luther rattled an ossified commotion on the table until she came back. He threw the tablet at her.

"I MEAN it. I'm cold," she read. She stared at the rattletrap old man. "Cold cold, not heartless cold?"

He nodded himself into a tockety tizzy.

"Well all right then, you old ghoul. I'll get you something to warm you up hotter than Hades and cremation, but then you've got to go back under."

Luther gestured toward the tablet and Carol Jean set it down on the table.

"I never liked it here anyway," he wrote.

Carol Jean brought Luther four jackets, two union suits, twelve well-mended and very clean shirts, sixteen pairs of socks and four comforters and bundled him up. Then she called Augustus. By dusk Luther Shedd was back in his earthy bed, and Carol Jean had arranged for a new headstone which read: Het Up and Back Under.

After Luther was reinterred and the new stone had been set, Carol Jean liked to take her evening walks there. She liked confirming that Luther was staying put, and she liked the old cemetery with its lichened stones and blackberry brambles, top-heavy daisies and perky buttercups, and the carved images of the stonework: weeping willows, winged skulls, funereal urns, and hands with their forefingers pointed skyward. Most of them, anyway. Not Luther's, of course. Carol Jean had arranged to have his hand chiseled with the finger pointing dead down. It was a moment of meanness, she knew. But she indulged it. She came by it naturally, courtesy of Luther who at this very moment, just to be contrary, was pulling down daisies. Some people just never change.

Second Nature

*Nature's laws affirm instead of prohibit. If you
violate her laws you are your own prosecuting
attorney, judge, jury, and hangman.*
                              —Luther Burbank

As long as I can remember there's been Chassures. As long as my
dad can remember, too. And probably his dad before him. It
wouldn't surprise me if you told me Chassures was here before the
land was. Chassures is one of the oldest families in town. We're
another. If you climb high enough in the family tree, Chassures and
Lacroys cross branches at Amy Trudo, which means we're cousins.
But, even though Chassures and Lacroys are related, it don't mean
they're alike. From the earliest time I can squint back at, my dad's
been saying, "He's a Chassure," as if it covered all kinds of hell. He
said it so often, in fact, that sometimes I thought Chassure wasn't a
last name. Chassure meant trouble, and the family was named after
it. Saying "He's a Chassure" was like saying "He's a caution," only it
cleared more dangerous ground. When my uncle, John Paul, got
drunk on a fishing trip up to Champlain and tried to prove he
could walk on water, my dad fished him out and said, "He's a
Chassure." When Ruby delivered her own baby in the '57 Willys
because Ron (that's her husband) was too drunk to drive her to the
hospital in Randolph, Dad said, "She's a Chassure," just like he said
it when old Coalie wrapped his new Ford pickup round a tree and
only an hour and a half later Ron spotted him flirting with the waitress at the Tally-Ho diner at the bus station over to White River. So
we were saying "He's a Chassure" for a long time before the accident
with Wayne come along. My dad says Chassure trouble flows way
back; it's in the blood.

Chassures and Lacroys always have been different. For one thing,
Lacroys is hill dwellers. Chassures, on the other hand, live low
down—in the woods or valleys. Not that living on a hill proves

you're smart. The north wind can sniff you out on a hill, rattle your windows, claw at your doors. It's some cold. Even with a furnace, you'll burn an extra cord a winter easy. But hills are pretty, too. Pretty tough, and pretty pretty. You stand back away from town. You see everything goes on—from the fog creeping on its river snake-belly in the morning to the sun sliding like a sled down the hill at night. Chassures, though, live in the woods, which makes sense, 'cause Chassures is mostly loggers, while Lacroys is mostly carpenters. And Chassures are natural hunters. They know their forests like most men know their own names and addresses. My dad likes to joke that sometimes Chassures can't see the trees for the forest. You can laugh, but nobody laughs around a Chassure with a gun, not even Lacroys. Lacroys hunt, but not like Chassures, not like it's second nature.

Chassure men take their buck every season. Wayne's camp was so covered with racks, it quilled like a porcupine. No matter which Chassure house you're at—Wayne's, Billy's—there'll be skins drying, waiting to be sold.

Even my father admits they can hunt. But he says a Chassure couldn't drive a nail straight with a ruler. They aren't too handy with a chain saw neither. Wayne cut his arm off limbing a tree. That's the way with Chassures; they practically been logging since before there was wood. Still, something's always going wrong. Wayne never seemed to miss his arm. He's a better hunter with one arm than most men are with two. Wayne wasn't a show-off about it; he was just good. It was Wayne first took me hunting.

I was ten when Wayne first took me out. The first time he guided me around and showed me deer sign. Spoor. Paths to the brook. A spot beneath some evergreens all beaten down where one had slept. It's strange how you can live in a place, walk through these woods, and never even know what you are seeing. I'd been sleepwalking all my life. So much meaning in a bent twig.

At the blind Wayne poured me a cup of coffee. I warmed my hands on the thermos mug and watched Wayne fuss with the blind, reweaving branches, checking the wind. "Two paths cross here," he said, "one to the salt lick, other to the brook." He picked his teeth with a twig. "It's a good spot."

I nodded, feeling the steam of the coffee on my face.

Wayne didn't talk much. Dad said Chassures never talked much unless they were drunk, and then they talked too damn much. Wayne must've done all his talking in high school. Everybody in town told some Wayne story—like the time he borrowed Ed Lacroy's tractor to go home after Ed's daughter got married. So drunk, he lost the tractor. From the ruts dug in the road, it looked like he got stuck on Sugar Maple Hill and rocked her right over a bank. Wayne walked away, but the tractor didn't live to tell about it. They found her totaled at the bottom of the gully.

He raised some hell with the Hall girls, too. Sisters, if you can get a handle on that. Linda and Sandy. If you believe what people say, he got them both bred. He was going with one of the Hall girls when he lost his arm.

During duck season, Wayne asked me, "You hear stories about me?" When I nodded, Wayne cocked the butt of the Winchester against his hipbone. "I'll just tell you once. When you're in high school you'll know it's true. There's nothing to do around here," he said, "so you have to raise your own hell or heaven. Understand?"

I nodded. Wayne never had any trouble talking to me.

Lacroys helped Wayne raise his house when he turned eighteen, a log cabin built below his brother Billy's in a stand of birches. Wayne spent a lot of time there, especially after he lost his arm and the second Hall girl. Alone except for his beagles, Frank and Jesse. Aside from them and the woods, Wayne was alone most the time.

If I had to be alone, I'd choose the hills any day. A forest can get to you. It's always talking—rubbing its branches together, creaking like old bones. It hides a lot, too: moss, and springs, empty birds' nests, a bat cave full of skeletons, tumble-down chimneys. Woods are like somebody who's always jawboning to keep you from asking questions, to keep you from their secrets. Give me hills where you can see clear—wide meadows.

Years ago, Lacroys cleared these hills for farming like it was easy as shaving. Hay fields, orchards, summer gardens clipped back the borders of the woods. Lacroys were farmers. Chassures, though, were loggers and, before that, trappers. My dad says they'd help out with the farming, getting in the hay before a storm, or finding strays in the far pastures at milking time, but Chassures didn't take to it like Lacroys.

My dad sold the Lacroy farm about ten years ago. More money in land than in farming. He kept the hillside acres for family. His brothers each got a parcel to build on. People from away bought up the rest.

Our town's changed a lot. Wayne said it was on account of the out-a-staters. He said our town's got out-a-staters like a barn's got rats. I don't know about rats, but it is changing. There's only one working farm in town today, and that's Davis's. And he's not even local; 'come down from the Northeast Kingdom. And there are shops in the old wool mill—a silversmith, and an antique store, a store just for coffee, a pottery. Natives don't shop at the mill. Mostly transplants own it, and mostly tourists shop it.

Another change: years ago we used to get summer people, families who come up to swim and horse around, same families year after year. Most these families don't come up anymore. We still get out-a-staters, maybe more than ever, but they're just shussing through. They come up to ski in the winter or camp in the summer. In the fall there's leaf peepers or hunters. Wayne said they come up to look down on us, to laugh at us. A bunch of hicks. He said looking down at us made people feel good. If Wayne saw a New Jersey license plate parked in front of Shaw's General Store, he wouldn't go in. He'd stand outside leaning against the car, working at his teeth with a toothpick or twig, peering out from under his NRA cap, his face in half-shadow like our hill when the sun slips.

Wayne wasn't what you'd call good-looking. Chassures were not big men. When they attacked a forest with their chain saws and rigs, they looked more like beavers than Paul Bunyans. But damn, they were quick. When they finished a day's work, the forest would look like a stubble of fall beard. They were quick and sure spoilers, if not the most graceful with a saw.

Being a Chassure, Wayne weren't too tall. And his left sleeve flapped like a flannel ghost. He never bothered to roll it up. His clothes looked borrowed. Too big. Too small, or new, not broken in. Even his teeth didn't look like his own. Stained with the

Redman he chewed, they looked like an old man's teeth, teeth as old as headstones. With one arm, chewing was easier than smoking—nothing to light. In winter, Wayne wore his beard long like a scarf. My dad said Chassures look like a pack of hillbillies in the winter, but Wayne said a beard's nature's way to keep warm.

Wayne's hair length matched whatever length of time he'd been up to the cabin alone. More than a month, it curled over his collar. Shorter, it cleared his neck. His hair was dark as summer pine shadows. But his eyes were pale blue. Most Chassures have blue eyes, pale as mirrors. All outside, no inside, they turned the world around. Not much you could read there.

One of the first seasons Wayne took me out hunting, he said, "If you treat your gun with respect, she'll treat you good. Like a woman."

I could feel a laugh building up in me. I couldn't see how Wayne, with his one arm and no girlfriend, no wife, and two bastard kids, could pretend to know anything about women. But when I saw myself in his silver-blue eyes, the laugh withered inside me. In a mirror things get all reversed, twisted around. It brought me up short.

There was a lot you couldn't know about Wayne. I never knew if he liked living here or not. He used to complain about the gossip. Most of it's tall tales, he said, and you spend the rest of your life living up or down to it. And once he lost his arm, he never seemed to have enough to do. He did odd jobs and puttered around the cabin. In the summer and fall he split wood, which took time with one arm. He'd tag along with his brothers to watch the logging. And he went hunting, of course, but he wasn't busy. He hung around Shaw's, poking at the tobacco stuck in his teeth, passing the time, or he kept to himself. He complained about having too much time to think. My dad said he could do more thinking and less drinking.

Wayne went a long time between drinks, but, once started, he drank himself stupid. Someone would cart him home. But he never drank when he was hunting. He'd have a Bud for lunch maybe, but that'd be it. When Chassures drink, they get wild-eyed, bedeviled.

Too bad Wayne didn't keep some mirrors handy when he drank; it might have kept him dry. But Wayne felt the time weigh on him heavily when he wasn't drinking. He had a TV, but it only got one channel. Reception's as bad in the valley as it is in the hills. And he never was much of a reader. He had nothing to do and too much time to do it in, so sometimes I suspect he felt trapped.

Other times I thought that he liked his life; it was all he knew, and he wasn't making plans to move. For all his complaining about the gossip, he didn't want the town history to change. He worried about the people from away, how they were trying to crowd us out, how things was changing. Whole state's being bought up and run by flatlanders, he said—which was partly true. No locals, except maybe Ed, who has a contracting business, could afford to buy land, let alone a business. But I think Wayne could have overlooked that if Ms. Schwarz hadn't stirred up gun control.

Ms. Schwarz ran one of the mill shops. Her sign read, "Buy a Piece of Vermont's Past—Antiques and Real Estate." Above that sign, another spelled the store's name: "History Repeats Itself." All the mill stores have clever names.

Wayne once cracked a joke about the name of her store. "I guess it's got a stutter," he said. But he didn't pay much mind. Wayne thought it was funny how all the people came up here from away to get away. "You can't get away from anything in a small town," he said, "past, present, or future. People are always watching, always talking."

Ms. Schwarz came here from New York. Like the other people in the mill, she held herself apart. She was friendly when she bumped into locals, but that didn't happen very often.

Gossip didn't nettle her like it did Wayne. I doubt it reached her. Wayne never mentioned her flat out—even after she hung the new sign in her store window after losing the picture one in her ridge house, "Make Vermont Safe—Support Gun Control."

Somebody'd fired within the safety zone after sunset. She had posted her property. That was her first mistake. When you grow up with the woods, you know they don't belong. Not to anyone. They belong to themselves. A hunter meets the woods however and wherever they happen to be. A buck don't read "NO TRESPASSING." And when a sign's between a gun and a buck, a hunter won't either.

He ignores it. If he reads it, he'll take exception to it, and he'll find some way of letting you know. You're better off not posting.

Ms. Schwarz's second mistake was hanging up the store sign. She should have glazed the window and let the incident pass. That's what a local would do. But she wasn't a local. If anybody in town knew who blew out her window, he weren't talking. Wayne never mentioned the gun control sign.

But I know he worried about it even before the sign went up. Wayne warned me about the new people. "They'll eat oats and bark," he said, "and tell you how all deer are Bambi. Before you know it, they'll take your guns away, take away the whole damn Constitution one right at a time. And when you're standing there empty-handed, left with nothing to fight with, nothing to fight for, they'll take over the country." The way he hefted his Winchester when he told me this, it looked for a moment like he'd grown a new arm where his stump used to be. He moved the gun that natural.

I didn't have my own gun then. I wasn't old enough yet, my dad said. Wayne agreed. The first time Wayne and I hiked up to his deer camp, he caught me sneaking a peek at the butt of his Winchester. Rubbed to a high shine, it caught the sun beautiful. Wayne chuckled, looking down at me. "Your time will come," he said. "A gun's a big responsibility. You have to grow into it."

Sometimes Wayne brought Frank and Jesse along. They nipped right along, picking up trails. Wayne said they was good deer hunters, except when you didn't fell the deer with the first hit. Blood crazed them. They got too yelpy. I saw what he meant come deer season. Drops of red blood burning into soft November snow. We didn't see Frank and Jesse until the next morning. They was running that deer, and it wasn't even Wayne's hit. Wayne said he felt sorry for that deer, running wounded. When they're wounded, they run wild, crashing into saplings, stone walls. They hurt themselves.

Sometimes at night now, I look out my window down the hill, down to about where I know Wayne's cabin is—brooding empty in the woods. And I think what an awful responsibility it is hunting down the truth. Sometimes whole sentences Wayne said belly-up in my memory like he was standing here saying them right now. And if the accident hadn't happened, maybe I wouldn't have remembered any of it, maybe I wouldn't have learned a thing—like the first time at camp Wayne let me hold the Winchester. He sat quiet, fiddling with a toothpick before he nodded at the rifle and said, "Pick it up." He watched me raise the rifle, then he said, "It feels a little like the first time you drive a car. You hold a gun, and you know there's a God, and you hope you're not in his sights." He wedged the toothpick between his thumb and index finger, flexing it. "All that power's got to make you shake, make you a little scared. And it's got to make you a little dizzy, a little hungry for it. If it don't do both, you got no business holding a gun at all." He snapped the toothpick in two.

Jeezum, he was right; I was shaking. I didn't even know if the gun was loaded. And I was surprised, too, because I'd never took Wayne for a religious man. My dad raised me Methodist, but we don't talk God outside of church, like it's bad manners for Methodists. Chassures are Presbyterian, so maybe it's okay for them. Dad says if you go back far enough, Chassures and Lacroys was both Catholic, but that must go as far back as time itself.

My hands trembled as I put the gun back in the corner where I got it, and I remember Wayne's head was bowed. He was looking down at his feet just like he was praying, or like he was ashamed.

These are the things I'm trying to remember, to add up, because Wayne wasn't always crazy, which you might think if you talked to some people now. He seemed normal enough. He came to the family picnics, ate, and drank a beer or two, same as everyone else. Only difference was he didn't talk as much as everybody else. But then he never did. He talked when he had to, or wanted to. He always had a word for Earl at the post office about the snow, or the drought, or whatever the weather was doing, and he always had a joke for Red at the store. So you have to sift through what you hear to get at the truth. Nobody's talking too much out in the open, though, 'cause Chassures is an old family. If people mention it at all, they're careful to call it "the accident."

Wayne said there's two kinds of gossip—public-domain gossip, which is the kind of busybody gossip that means people secretly envy you, maybe even admire you, and behind-closed-doors gossip, which is the serious kind and means they out-and-out fear you. Both do their damage.

Ms. Schwarz was the first kind of gossip when she got the chance. Even though she didn't really belong, if she bumped into you at Shaw's, she'd pin you down with questions about who made Honor Roll, or whose father did what for a living. Red thought she was just a nosybody trying to drum up local business. But Earl over at the post office thought she was real nice to take an interest in the town. He had to eat his words later. But I could see why Earl liked her. No question, Ms. Schwarz was what Wayne called a real fox. Odd though, Wayne never seemed to see her. If she chanced by, his body'd go all limp on itself like it was shriveling into his shirt, and he'd pull his smile in behind those mirror eyes of his. If she tried to fix Wayne with a couple questions in the store, he'd just grunt something and turn sharp, his loose sleeve snapping as he spun round. He didn't have much time for outsiders.

It didn't strike me at the time, but I've thought about it since, because Wayne believed standing outside a little, being a stranger, helped make you a better hunter. A deer is so much a part of the forest, he said, that sometimes a deer itself doesn't know what it's going to do. It just runs, acting out the will of the woods. And sometimes Wayne did know what a deer was going to do better than the deer did. If the deer thrashed west toward the lick, Wayne'd sneak off east toward the brook, or he'd just stand still, and, like he'd read the deer's mind, sure enough the deer more times than not would wind up in Wayne's range. I thought it was spooky, but Wayne said it was just that he saw the forest with a tourist's eyes. Like a stranger, he watched the woods, what the animals did, where they went, what they ate, when they slept, just like they was foreigners. But, because he didn't know the language, he did not and could not know why they did what they did. Wayne said, for a hunter, this was a great advantage. "The whys will just muddle you, 'cause you might guess wrong. You need facts and actions to be a good hunter, not guesses or causes. A deer will outrun guesswork every time."

I made a study of everything Wayne said. At night before I fell asleep, I'd go over and over what he told me. I never listened so hard to anyone. I'd gone out with my dad before, but it wasn't the same as Wayne, because my dad, to tell the truth, had never taken a buck—at least in my lifetime. He told of taking a six-pointer when he was eighteen. But it's sport with my father. It's more like school with Wayne. And I wanted to be a good hunter; I really did. But my first chance, I failed.

Wayne and me gone duck hunting down to Bule's Bog. A perfect day, crisp as a Macintosh, the sky daring you to imagine a deeper blue. Wayne was leaning against a rock, his hands in his hunting gloves resting easy on his rifle. I breathed deep, and I couldn't imagine anything better than this. God's country, Wayne called it. And then I heard them so far above, calling to each other clear as this air, this day, nudging fall a day forward, tugging the winter down from Canada behind them. A perfect V of geese, sun glinting off their wings. The sky rang with their voices. It felt good, like school before vacation, like something was about to change. And then I heard the shot, saw a shape fall from the sky, a dark stone. A dead thing. "Jeezum," I yelled, jumping all over myself and soaking my jacket, "you got her." Frank and Jesse yapped and splashed. When they come back, Jesse led the way. When he laid down the mess of bloody feathers, I lowered my eyes. A crumpled Schlitz can bobbed in the marsh grass.

I couldn't look at Wayne. There he'd let fly with a perfect hit— the best, the first, really, I ever seen—and I couldn't find a thought. I could feel the heat rising off my cheeks. I was proud of him, and envious, maybe even angry. I still don't know. But I found nothing to say. I cursed myself secretly, called myself "pantywaist, sissy." But I had no words.

Wayne smiled at me and said, "It's okay. A lot of people fall dumb the first time."

I knew Wayne had never been shook dumb, but I let it go.

"That's the first time," he said, "but the second or third time you realize the woods is a circle of power, and, in that circle, death only matters as food for the living. Nobody cries when a mouse dies, 'cause the owl's going to eat, going to live another day. You don't hurt for the weak, because you're happy for the strong. And if the strong have eaten, they won't come looking at you like you're the next meal."

We ate goose for dinner that night, but I didn't savor it. Wayne would fault me, but I've always felt sorry for weak things. I beat a snake near to death once, because I caught it with the hind legs of a mouse sticking out of its jaws. When I pulled the mouse free, its head was gone. Wayne says weakness brings out the ugliness in other animals. It's nature's law; there's no such thing as pity. A broken wing, a missing leg means only easy prey. "The meek inherit the earth all right. They're buried in it."

When Wayne first started going spooky, I didn't much notice. The days chased each other like they always do. We stopped at Shaw's to pick up a tin of Redman and chew the fat awhile. Wayne'd buy me a birch beer and straddle the chair by the counter. Red would settle against the counter and quiz Wayne on the hunting. Where'd he take his buck this year? See any more sign? How his brothers doing with the logging? He heard they had trouble with the rig. Filling time with questions he already knew the answers to.

Sometimes Red would try to draw Wayne into politics, but he wouldn't go. He'd listen to Red go on about "That Iranian" or "The White House simps." But Wayne didn't participate unless the politics was local. If Red complained about transplants from New Jersey and Connecticut, Wayne nodded. If Red threatened, "Ain't nobody from away going to mess with my property. If I got to use my gun, well hell, then I'll use my gun," Wayne would nod and spit. Only after the door swung closed would he laugh and say, "Fat Red Shaw couldn't hit a dead moose with a frying pan. Honest to Pete." And he laughed so hard, he choked.

By spring the only talk in Shaw's was Ms. Schwarz's gun law. People were fired up. The store was crowded. Ms. Schwarz had been drumming up signatures for gun control and had even written letters to the governor in Montpelier. Channel 3 had sent somebody down to interview her. Even Earl at the post office was cranked up about it.

Wayne didn't seem ruffled at all. Maybe he thought it'd boil over. That's what my dad said. For a while it seemed he was right. Spring come and go. The Canada geese crossed overhead again. School let out, and summer drifted in on long days and short shadows. It wasn't until the fall that things reheated.

Somebody smashed Ms. Schwarz's window and trashed the place, tore the gun control sign to shreds and flushed some of her real estate listings down the hopper, clogging the pipes good. Red said the place was a mess. But nobody was caught. Looking back, I still don't think Wayne done it. It wasn't his style.

In Current Events, Mr. Glover, our social studies teacher, explained the meaning of referendums. He said we should talk to our parents 'cause, at town meeting, they were going to vote on a referendum. My dad said he wasn't going to waste his time on a work night listening to a bunch of fools talk themselves into a frenzy. So I got news from Red, who told me the meeting weren't too pleasant. Things got out of hand, a regular shouting match between the transplants and the natives. The lines were clear enough drawn, no mistaking.

During doe season, Wayne came into the store and asked me if I'd like to walk some trails. "Been a lot of activity at the lick."

We listened to the commotion over the referendum for a while. Red was saying how a midnight round outside a certain person's window might shift the balance of votes. Somebody else said how he'd like to shoot a few rounds right in Ms. Schwarz's bed, which raised a few hoots. Wayne chucked some coins on the counter for his chew and muttered, "Blowhards." He spit a gob on the top step of the porch.

That fall Wayne struck me as changed somehow. He moved the same. He joked the same, but there was something skittish about him. His hand hopped like something lurked behind every tree. "There's nothing dangerous in these woods," Wayne used to say, "but yourself." You wouldn't have thought it to look at him. Plain spooky, that jerky right hand. But otherwise Wayne was Wayne. His hair curled over his collar. He'd gotten a head start on his winter beard. But he seemed himself.

Before the end of deer season, he invited me to stay for supper at the cabin. He thawed some of last year's venison and fried it up with onions and potatoes. It was delicious, wild-tasting and smoky.

After supper, Wayne tilted back in his rocker and set to work with a toothpick. It was quiet except for the woodstove hissing and the occasional scritch of a field mouse in the ceiling socking away some seed for the winter.

"It's good to have company," Wayne said. "Too much nature can get to you."

When I didn't answer, he went on. "You ever hear those peepers on a summer night, buzzing away?"

I nodded.

"Sometimes that buzz gets so loud, it begins to take over everything. It begins to sound like the only thing left in the world. If you aren't careful, it'll suck you right inside it."

My skin prickled gooseflesh, like someone run a fingernail over my spine. Chalk screeching on a blackboard. But Wayne just rocked back and forth, toothpick clenched in his teeth. His eyes reflected air, empty space, nothing at all.

"Seth,"—he called my name so sudden I almost upset my chair. "Seth, a small town isn't right for everybody. Some people it fit like a second skin. Take Red. Small town's like a damn birthday suit for Red. But on other people it fits like secondhand clothes. Too tight, like you can't breathe. I'm that kind. That's why I like to spend my time out here."

I nodded and slid my hand under my thigh to warm it.

"But you have to be careful in the woods, too," Wayne said, "'cause they can be tricky. Sometimes when you get outside—not a house as far as you can see—you think this is a big country, that you're free as you want to be. It's not true. Maybe it was once, but it's not true anymore, 'cause everywhere you look there's a foreigner just waiting to rob your rights."

I tuned Wayne out there. He was beginning to find a foreigner, New Jerseyite or New Yorker, behind every tree. This church phrase popped into my head: you're not your brother's keeper. I wasn't. But I was beginning to think Wayne might need a keeper. While he rambled on, I tried to remember me and Wayne at the deer camp talking late into the night, drinking coffee, playing poker for matchsticks—all the things my dad wouldn't let me do—how, when we walked the woods, Wayne let me scout. He named me Aquila after the constellation, because he said I had eagle eyes. I didn't miss much.

Wayne taught me all the constellations. One night after supper, we walked up Christian Hill to the old overgrown cemetery and laid down. The night pressed clean against our faces. I don't think I ever seen as many stars as that night. At first they just seemed to be dumped there haphazard as sand at the beach, but Wayne drew his finger against the sky and showed me how they all connected in lines until they fell into place in the design. Pegasus, the flying horse. Cygnus, the swan, and Aquila, the eagle. Wayne wrapped his hand around mine and traced them out. We spoke hushed. Wayne said that men should only hunt by moonlight. That way only the men who knew what they were after would hunt. The others, the ones who hunt by accident, would fall by the wayside. The hill rose hard beneath our backs, and the darkness gathered holy as shadows in church.

Remembering this, I felt better about Wayne. I drifted back into the conversation. He was talking about hunting.

"Hunting doesn't come to me second nature. It comes to me first nature." He laughed. "It's the way I am, not the way I fit myself in."

My skin pricked again. It sounded like gibberish. As soon as I spotted a hole in the conversation, I said good-night. It would be the last time I'd talk to Wayne. That sentence lived to haunt me, and I've mulled it over since: there's nature that is simply the way you are. And there's nature that's everything—the circle of power and the hill, the deer, and the brook. The whole design. And there's second nature—the way you naturally fit yourself into the design. You can go on and on if you begin to think like Wayne. Sometimes I think if only I'd listened more carefully I might have been able to prevent what happened; I might have made a difference.

I couldn't know then that was Wayne's last deer season. He never even took a buck that year. First time, too. After that supper, I avoided him, soured on going to the cabin. I didn't stop off at Shaw's after school anymore. I kept busy enough so I didn't miss him. School ended again. The commotion over the referendum blew over like dad said it would. Nothing happened. I got my first job pumping gas at the minimart that summer and me and Gary Lacroy rebuilt the engine on his father's old jeep. Fall swung round. And I didn't think much about Wayne. It was only September. Deer season wasn't for a month yet. School was beginning again. I can only piece the rest of it together from what people said, and it is a crazy quilt when you're done.

One morning in September, Wayne hiked into Shaw's and bought some tobacco. Wayne had the Winchester with him. He told Red he wanted it clean as water by deer season. He wanted his buck in time for Thanksgiving that year. Red thought he acted odd, a little shack-wacky. "Hunting season's weeks off yet, Wayne," Red told him. Wayne grinned and said he was just getting the feel of it. Then Red wondered if he'd been drinking. He smelled like he was sweating whiskey. While Wayne tucked some tobacco against his gums, his eyes wandered over to the newspaper rack, skimmed an article about how some Connecticut developers wanted to flood the valley to generate cheaper power to expand the ski areas down south.

Wayne should not have read that newspaper. I'd never known him to even read the funnies. In our town, we live outside of news. We haven't had a local paper in my lifetime. The nearest papers—there's three—are published in the nearest cities, and, if you drew a circle around us, they'd all fall more than sixty miles from the center. It's not our news. It's not that we live in the past. It's more like we live outside of time altogether, in no particular time at all. That's why Wayne never should have noticed that paper. He might not have except Red made some fool comment about how the flatlanders weren't even being coy anymore, how they were flooding us out of our homes and bragging about it. Wayne still said nothing.

Then Red told him how Ms. Schwarz was getting busy again, this time going into the school auditoriums to pitch gun control to the kids. When Red retells it, he shakes his head here. But Wayne still said nothing. He paid for his Redman, tucked his tobacco pouch in the pocket of his hunting jacket, and left.

Nobody knows any more until they heard the shot. There was no more preparation than that. The three minutes between Shaw's and the mill, the few steps separating them. Whatever distance Wayne covered in those three minutes, he covered outside of distance, outside of time. Earl found Wayne in the corner of Ms. Schwarz's shop, the butt of the Winchester propped against his belly, his hand on the barrel, Ms. Schwarz, face down on the floor. Earl says he didn't see the blood right away. When the police turned her over, they found one neat bullet hole dead center in her forehead.

My father heard the whole story at Shaw's on his way home from work. When he came inside, he said, "He's a Chassure." My knees ran watery; I felt like every muscle in my body was crying. And I ran outside.

The cold air hit my face like a slap, but I climbed Christian Hill. When I reached the top, I crumpled like the dead leaves and stared at the sky. Stars endless as snowflakes in a blizzard. All unlike, a ragtag confusion as pointless and as empty as a circle.

A woman is dead. A man is in prison. Those are the simple facts of it. I could count the reasons like stars until I'm dead and never come to the end, never know any more than I do today. But I know saying "He's a Chassure" doesn't get you very far, brings you up short and nowhere at all. I know that much.

The newspaper people are swarming our town. They want to interview Wayne in jail, but he isn't talking. Before his lawyer told him not to talk to anyone, Wayne said he was sorry for dragging the family into it, that he'd acted on his own, in the best interests of his country. He tried to keep us out of it. He asked that I take care of Frank and Jesse. Wayne only wrote me once from prison to tell me I could have the Winchester while he was gone. But the police kept the gun. I never once fired the Winchester, but I got my own gun now; I guess I'll get my chance.

The town's tight-lipped about the accident. Chassures is an old family. Nobody wants to drag them down. The deer camp's boarded up. The cabin's closed, water and electric shut off. Red, who wouldn't know enough to shut his mouth in a flood, said Wayne swiped a fork in prison and dug his own eyes out. I don't believe it's true.

When it's full moon, and the silver light falls like sugar snow in February, I hear Frank and Jesse howling. I know what they're barking at—slipping out of time. Sometimes in the winter, when you're lying on your bed and you look at a green balsam against a blue sky, you'd swear the sky had fallen right out of summer.

Could be any month, any month at all. Slipping out of time, the seasons reversing. All order lost.

When I stand on our hill and look down into the valley, I note how it narrows. Every step forward you take, the closer the world is around you, the tighter your breath in your chest. My dad said, it's hard to believe, but when he was a boy, the whole town was meadowland—hand-cleared by him and my grandparents and great-grandparents for farmland. Now the woods are reclaiming it. In a few years, we'll have to clear-cut or we're going to lose our view.

At night I hear the pines whispering to each other, to the north wind. Sometimes I hear the plop of a cone dropping on the soft rot of pine needles. The trees are laughing at us. Their branches are shaking free. Seeds fly. Underground, roots creep, pushing toward the house. I'm afraid to fall asleep. The woods are closing in. "We're closing in," they say. One of these days, before it's too late, I'm moving away from here. I'm keeping to the hills.

⌒ The Anecdote of the Island ⌒

When the thick o' fog rolls in, socking you in for days, sometimes weeks, you shrug. You may even be happy. The fog makes you more lonely or less lonely. You do not know which. But you know that the day sailors, picnickers, throttle jockeys won't be tying up, won't be hailing the Whaler for a motor from the mooring. Until the fog slouches out to sea, you will be alone, more alone than usual.

You pound down vodka, keep the bottle handy, wedged into the waistband of your shorts. You roam the beach, hear the swash and backwash of the sea, which you can't see, which you can only sense, rolling up against you, ineluctable, perpetual. A wheel of water in a U-shaped trough. Your feet are tough. You pad barefoot over rockweed, eelgrass, aluminum flip-tabs, rock, and shell, fog so close it seems to be condensing on your skin from within. The fog throws up carcasses in sudden high relief on the beach. Remains of some crow-ravaged mammal. Fur, stiff and mangy with salt. Rabbit? Cat? Dead animal has no legs. A cormorant flies up next into your vision; its pure white alar bones poke through the drying skin, the mangles of black feather. A small but bottomless hole reminds itself where his keen eye has been. You sight through one eye and out the other. White sand. White fog. Whistling reed of air. You step carefully over the black spans fanning the beach. You follow the taxonomy of the strand: fish bones. Sand fleas. Snails. And worms.

In silver drizzles, you smoke cigarettes. You like smoking outside the bunkhouse where beads of water unthread from the needles of the Scotch pine, slide, drop, and meet your hot ash with a hiss. The fog does not lift; it just back-and-fills, swells, rakes itself into columns and re-forms. Air is indistinguishable from water. All elements, one. You wallow in your slug ease. Swallow some vodka. Water mats your coarse hair, braids it into dreadlocks. Your coiled head is a nest of snakes.

When the vodka bottle is empty, you sometimes hurl it into the foggy water. It depends on how empty the bottle is. But whether you hurl the bottle or scrape off the label with your hunting knife for the recycle bin, it makes no difference. The bottle always comes back.

You sit on the ledges. You brood, or you would be brooding if you could. But you're not that thoughtful. You are the state before a state of being, an empty space, a state of being before grace. Your eyes are periwinkles. Your fingers, razor clams. Your heart a clutch of unhinged mussel shells.

You cross these paths—beach to bunkhouse to beach to out-house to bunkhouse to main house. When you are drunk enough to realize that you are drunk, you like to walk through the main house. It sits high enough on the bluff that the sea sounds surge up. The house talks in tongues. To remind yourself that you have a voice, you holler as you walk. Hoots. Whoops. Banshee gibber-ish. You scream yourself hoarse, either because no one will hear you or because someone might. If a deranged ranger screams himself senseless and no one is there to hear it . . .

You enter the main house and light a cigarette in the room with the compass on the floor and stare down the fog. Below, the foghorns low, so low the sound might come from your throat. The boats moan so that they can hear themselves, so that they will know that they are still there. You moan back with the sound of wind keening over the mouth of an empty bottle.

The parlor idles, dark with the smell of summer houses: mildew, dry rot, dust, fly wings, mouse nest. The smell of time hung in a closet. A falcon, osprey, owl, and hawk glare glass-eyed at you from their perches on the fieldstone mantle. Their arranged deaths arrest them in bedraggled eternities—about to fly, about to land, about to prey. Heads rotated or cocked, wings bowed or bent or trimmed, tail feathers tilted or tucked and only slightly time-molted, weather wearied.

You open the cabinet for the lemon oil and chamois, rub the surfaces of tables and breakfronts, arms of rocking chairs with tenderness, trying to work moisture back into the grain. When you are drunk, when you are alone, this is your pleasure—the ache in the small of your back, the lemon tang undercut by the sweetness of the oil, the pump of your arms, the slick on your palms, the repeating circles rehearsing the firmness of maple and oak, mahogany and pumpkin pine. While the fog snuffles the window panes, wisps mouse-tail up the stairs, you polish, room by room, the furniture in the parlor, the children's alcoves, the commodore's master bedroom. The walls of the bedrooms are wooden, unadorned. Their plainness pleases you. They are dark. Their framing exposed, uprights wedge their ribs between floor and ceiling. The house is a skeleton of itself.

You enjoy opening drawers, cupboards, although, by now, you know what is there. A Parcheesi game. Picture books. Nursery rhymes. Well-greased playing cards. Cribbage boards, collar studs, cuff links, fishhooks, missing buttons. The cupboard doors open onto short corridors of time. Something about the house always feels startled. Time interrupted. Any minute the children could come tumbling back from the boat run aground, the thunderstorm, the beached whale, the small peril that summoned them, that rippled time. Any minute the children could resume the Parcheesi game, the hand of Old Maid. Any minute the commodore will parallel plot a course on the chart table. The quotidian habits dangle, wait for hands. Dog-eared pages, knitting needles with dropped stitches, cribbage boards, and dice wait for leisure to resume. You observe the book lice on the blue and red spines of the library books. Particle by particle, as slow as time passing, they devour the books. You think, *Eat your words.*

The kitchen is the only room where you are unwelcome. Cold stoves. Rusted pump handles. Dinged, black-bottomed kettles. Haunted by its uselessness, by the female ghosts of its clatter, dishes stacking and unstacking, whisks beating, kettles whistling, a teacup merrily shattering. It is the only room in the house that minds its loneliness. You feel large in its unpeopled spaciousness, its steel reflecting surfaces. You go there seldom. It smells sudsy and sour, the residue in laundry tubs, the mineral scale in the drainpipes.

Sometimes you lie on the beach, drunk and hopeful that sand and salt can scour you shell-clean of your human meat. But you sober up. You know better. Hope is hangover queasy. Once, you find a seal carcass on the beach, watch the flies attack the gashes in its blubber, wonder how long you would have to sit there to watch it rot clean away. Decomposition orchestrates a slow music.

You never sleep in the commodore's cottage. In part because you would not know which room to sleep in. In the fog one night you sit on the beach, pondering which room you would sleep in. You pass out. When a wave breaks on your face, you wake up. The bottle you'd tucked beneath your arm has washed away. You think of messages in bottles, the corked perfume bottles you tossed with your aunt into Boston Bay. Long ago. In the morning, you find the vodka bottle smashed against the rocks, sheared into beautiful convex triangles.

You sleep in the bunkhouse. At night, you choose not to dream. You sleep with two pillows, not to make a partner seem possible, but to make the bed seem larger, emptier.

There is a woman. When there is no fog, she chugs over in her converted lobster boat. She brings you baked goods. She cooks for you. She blows you. She makes a decent fish chowder. You think that she is pathetic, coming out to Eagle to give blowjobs to some lush who obviously doesn't give a damn. But you don't have the heart to tell her. Eventually, she figures it out herself. You miss the fish chowder.

You have few fears—the kitchen (but that's deeper than fear), running out of booze, and the cisterns. You run out of vodka one squally night. You usually ration carefully; you're surprised. Probably didn't count the flotsam bottle smashed on the rocks. You can't make it. You decide to head for Mackerel Cove. They'll have beer, wine, cigarettes.

When you enter the store, the tuna fishermen glance up. They're waiting out the storm, playing poker. They watch you without raising their eyes from their hands, watch as you thud down two cases on the counter, grab a carton of Kools, shed puddles of water on the floor.

One rearranges his hand and asks, "Where you cross from?"

"Eagle." The word feels strange in your mouth. Your tongue probes the hole left by the word, a missing tooth, a place that is not here. "Eagle," you repeat. You are a barnacle who talks.

He nods. The storm pelts the windows, screams the waves into furies. The men return to their cards. Their silence is approval. You're only an asshole if you don't make it. You always make it.

The beer shortens the trip back. You haul the beer up to the front room in the cottage, sit on one case while, bottle by bottle, you down the other. You like it here. A place outside of time. The house has accumulated so much past that, heavy with days, it falls through the rotted floor of itself. Out of time. You watch the rain and sea spray streak the glass, blear and trickle over the darkness beyond. Very little to fear. You listen to the storm, watch the water drip from your hair, sheet down your skins. You already lost everything. Wife. Home. Child. Lover. Maybe you did not lose them. Maybe you never wanted them in the first place. You do not favor connections. What is there left to fear?

You fear the cisterns. Not for yourself, but for the children who motor out on sunny days. You worry that one will test the rotted timbers, fall through into the circular darkness, arms broken, a bird with a useless wing. A voice in that cylindrical darkness. You worry that you will not see the child fall, will not hear his cries, that he will die slowly in that rubbled darkness where the Pearys used to store their coal. A cobbled coal floor. An enclosed exhausted sootiness. A pink-eyed rat. The cold that might have been heat. A child crying.

Those are your only fears. You've been streamlining for years, simplifying your life, no fears, no attachments, few pleasures—a bottle, cigarettes, fish chowder, and fog, the fog that is a shade of the night in your heart, only wetter, whiter. It is enough.

When the fog finally stirs, creeps off across the water, the sun returns, the boaters return, and you put away your bottle. You are a voice in your own head as you cleat and uncleat boats, patrol the beach, spike trash on a stick. You pace. You wait for fog.

Instead a sailboat scuds in, banging into the wharf, sails luffing and flapping. The sailor curses, kicks a fender. He wears a Greek fisherman's cap. He is neither Greek nor a fisherman. He is, you decide, an asshole. Strangling wine bottles in their hands, the crew pours out of the Sabre. Only then you see her, sitting aft, very still. She won't acknowledge you. She won't even glance at you. You are a handsome man, and her indifference roots you. Her hair is shag wing black. She wears a visored cap; her face scowls in the shadow. She is angry. You surmise that the clown tangling himself up in the sheets is her husband. You'd be angry, too. You stare at her without staring. Her white shorts are smudged with fish scale. Her skin is ruddy brown. Her breasts are small, nestlike. When she raises her eyes, her grass green eyes, you startle. Why do you note her? Why is this moment discrete? Why is it defining itself as separate from the moment-after-moment movement that makes day follow day, week follow week? Something about her beauty, her anger, touches you, and you crave her look. But she does not look. She stares at some middle distance where she is alone. You recover. You help her husband.

Near sunset, when her party leaves, you feel a pang that you cannot identify as regret. You want to love this woman. She seems possible somehow, perhaps because she is impossible. You watch their boat diminish. Life seems like this when there is no fog: a concatenation of just-missed alterities, the other life, the life that might have been.

When the fog returns, settles back into your hollows, you polish the furniture, feeling her too-green eyes on your back. Her face shimmers in the punts of your bottles. Her cool stare chills the piney air where you smoke and wait for the ash to hiss. You begin to think that you have invented her. Her green eyes are incredible. Her face develops in memory until it is sharper than her face. You are cursed with memory and time. You rub her image into the wood grains.

When we meet eight years later, you will insist that I am she. You have turned our anterior meeting into one of your stories. You have many. It's possible. Yes, I was there. But you may have invented the rest. You may, after all, have invented me. I cannot know. But if—if it were true, that you glimpsed me on a day like every other sad day of my former marriage; if, sailing, my husband and I stopped to picnic at Eagle as we often did; if I was angry; if you looked at me and found me beautiful, thought perhaps love was possible; if, departing, I remained in the wake of your following thoughts, what would it change? Twice, you let me slip away. Twice you set me on my way.

You helped my then-husband uncleat his sailboat. You stared as I diminished. Eight years later, you avert your eyes again from the possible life. We sit on the foot of my bed, watching the sun smolder red through fog. You will not tell me that you love me, perhaps because you don't, perhaps because you do. But you will not leave her. You will not come with me. After a year of debate, it conduces to this: I watch you leave as you once watched me. Our cars separate at the base of a hill. You diminish into a speck in my rearview mirror. When I look for you, I stare into my own eyes looking for you. And I begin to think that what you want is not love but the hope for love. Its remoteness. Its shadow self. You linger in dark places.

When we separate for the last time, I remember your anecdote, the one you told me at school the summer we met. A tourist asked you, "Is this really an island?"

Playing the Mainer, you answered, "It is if you stand on the mainland."

Wherever you stand, you are enisled. You no longer drink. You live on the mainland now with the woman who fills in the gaps in time. You tell me that you do not love her; you tell her that you do. But no matter where you live, I see you most at ease smoking beneath a Scotch pine and waiting for the hiss. Instead you spend your days now filling chairs, staring at the middle distance.

Far from you, preparing for my classes, I read a line from Barthes: "Boredom is not far from bliss: it is bliss seen from the shores of pleasure."

Wherever you are, you are quiet. I love you still.

Women's Problems

I've had better weeks. I should have been suspicious when I woke up Monday morning. Sleet tapped against the window. David had slept through the alarm again and snored beside me. Mr. Coffee spat boiling water at me. The parakeet's cage needed changing; Tweety Bird was eating the flayed newspaper. But who had time? I punched in late and out early.

After work, I went to see her in the hospital. She was sleeping. I counted the bubbles in her IV bottle and inhaled the chemically clean air until I fainted. Someone wheeled me out of her room on a gurney. Someone ripped my clothes off to help me breathe. In Recovery, I opened my eyes. The young man leaning over me— a doctor, I guessed, an intern—explained, "You hyperventilated." "Thank you," I said. My underpants stretched black over my abdomen like a censor's bar, a red heart on the hip, embroidered, "Saturday."

It was Monday. The shot elastic tickled my thigh. The sheet barely covered the hole in the side seam. She always warned me that this would happen. "It's to die for"—my mother's expression for embarrassment. To die for: I hated that expression. At least I had medical insurance. She couldn't fault me for that. I was covered.

On Tuesday, a man tried to rape me. I was wearing a tight skirt, or maybe it was my eye shadow. I may have shaded my eyes too heavily. I hadn't been as careful lately, as subtle. I'd been avoiding mirrors. As I boarded the bus, I felt a hand move between my legs. I felt another hand, cold as murder, move in my stomach.

Silently, I appealed to the bus driver; he averted his eyes. I pivoted, cocked my leg, and kicked, spiking with my heel. I heard someone howling. I never saw his face. I dropped two quarters in the coin slot and walked down the aisle. The passengers draped newspapers over their faces. It must have been the eye shadow.

On Wednesday, David moved out. "I can't go on like this," he said. "You're never home. When you are home, you mope. When you mope, you don't cook. When you don't cook, you don't eat. When you don't eat, I don't eat. There's nothing to eat here."

He yanked the refrigerator door open. A ketchup bottle shivered against a jar of Dijon mustard. A few cups of post-dated yogurt. A shriveled root of ginger. I couldn't argue with him; there wasn't anything to eat. I nodded in agreement, hoping that I wasn't wearing too much eye makeup. It streaks when I cry. I hate messy good-byes.

"You need help," David counseled.

I nodded.

"I need something to eat," David said.

I nodded again. I thought of suggesting he roast his damn parakeet. The whim passed.

"Professional help," David said, his finger underlining the word, professional, in midair. "I don't know who's sicker," he added, "you or her."

I nodded again; I didn't know, either.

When he stomped out, he took his coat, but he left Tweety Bird. David must be staying at his mother's. He doesn't know anyone else in the city but his mother and me. He calls her Mummy. He used to call me Sylvester.

After he slammed the door and clomped down the stairs, I waited for a minute until the silence settled, then I walked to the 7-Eleven and bought some fresh yogurt. The Dannon people should stamp proverbs on the lids, words of wisdom, like those baked into fortune cookies: The way to a man's heart is through his stomach; Eat, drink, and be merry. Guidelines, simple guidelines. I tried to picture them: Somewhere in Chinatown, in the fortune factory, mothers, rows and rows of mothers, hunkered down over Smith-Coronas, typing tiny curls of paper, Salada tea tags, the fortunes in the How Much Do You Weigh? (Too Much) machine, typing their fingernails to the nubs, typing out the futures that their mothers typed, the futures that their mothers' mothers . . . David once said I was a victim of circular thinking.

When I got home, I opened the refrigerator door to put the yogurt away. The bulb had burned out. The rest of the week will be better.

On Thursday after work, I went to the hospital again. She was still sleeping. I counted bubbles in her IV bottle. I did not faint. Behind the curtain, her roommate watched the Newlywed Game, the new Newlywed Game, on the pay TV. "If your husband were a banana split, would you eat him with or without nuts?" the emcee asked. "With." Giggles. The roommate's curtain billowed, then hung still as windless July. Sleet pattered against the plate-glass window. Thermal pane. Inside, as always, humid and hot, drowsing temperature. Climate control. I never actually saw the roommate, but once a hand poked a box of chocolates through the curtain.

"Thank you," I said, removing an empty paper frill. (I don't eat chocolate.)

"'S okay," she said.

I crinkled the paper in my fingers. Sometimes I heard her whispering to her husband. I think that it was her husband. I wondered if she ever fed him chocolates.

The gooseneck lamp cast a halo on the hospital sheet. Her hand rested in the center of the light. I closed mine over hers. I felt the blood pulse in her veins.

"David moved out," I told her. Her arteries opened and closed. Her lungs filled. Her blood coursed.

"Why buy a cow when you can milk your neighbor's for free?" she had asked me when he moved in.

Dad milked the neighbor's cow and bought her. I haven't seen him since he remarried. I was five. He never gave me advice—only birthday cards. I've saved them all. Mom used to threaten to throw them away. "You can't keep bad milk," she said holding her nose. "It turns on you. Sours."

I had no milk at home in my dark refrigerator—only yogurt.

"Save it for marriage," she said, shaking the dust mop out the bedroom window.

"What," I asked. "Save what?"

"You know." A blizzard of dust kitties on the front lawn. "You know perfectly well. Save *it*."

Lately, David and I had been very thrifty. We hadn't *it*-ed for months, hadn't even thought about *it*-ing. He was too busy starving. I was too busy forgetting to buy groceries. He blamed my mother, her bad heart, for our problems. I attributed it all to lady luck, dumb luck. But we were as separate now as two halves of a fortune cookie.

When we got takeout, David would never eat fortune cookies. "Just flour and sugar," he said. "They're always stale."

"I think he's gone for good this time," I told her. Her hand still rested in the center of the circle. I wanted, for an instant, to grab it, bite it, scream in her face, "Tell me something, something you can't sum up in one sentence, something upside down or unjust, like, 'Good things do not come in small packages, do not come to she who waits.' Tell me anything, anything at all; tell me that I bite the hand that feeds me." But instead I kissed her good-bye, a small kiss on each fingertip. The tips tasted like vanilla.

The sheets on my unmade bed snarled me in a darkness as black as my hair. The bed was bigger than I'd remembered. It had been a while since I'd slept alone. Alone. But I woke up on Friday morning with my respect intact.

On Friday morning, I called in sick. "I'm sick," I lied to Carol, my supervisor.

"Look, Deirdre, I'm sympathetic. I really am," she said, "but this can't go on. It has to stop ASAP. You've been late or absent every day this month. Work can be a wonderful cure-all, take your mind off your troubles."

"I'm sick," I said. "Okay." She sighed. "But don't say I didn't warn you."

Idle hands are the devil's playthings.

A stitch in time saves nine.

Cleanliness is next to godliness.

I surveyed the apartment. What would she say, I wondered. *Nothing,* I answered. Her hand rested on a hospital sheet. A jar bubbled over her head.

I decided to look in the mirror. I crossed my eyes. I wanted two of me. Misery loves company. What if my eyes stuck that way? They were sticking. No one would ever love me, just as she had foretold. But by noon they had uncrossed. Thank God it's Friday. I ate a piña colada yogurt and threw out the ginger root.

I didn't sleep very well. The ax murderer called me at midnight.

On Saturday, he called my listed phone number again. He panted into my ear. I hung up. He called again at noon. I recognized his pant.

"David," I asked, "is that you?" When he didn't answer, I knew that it was the ax murderer.

So. He'd found my number at last—a single woman living alone, her name clearly printed in the white pages for all the ax murderers in the world to see. The vast network of ax murderers, greeting each other on the street, "Give Deirdre a call; she's in the book." But I did have a peephole. I could spot an ax murderer a hall's breadth away. What's that bulge in your jacket? Is that an ax, or are you happy to see me? It's tough concealing an ax under a pea coat, even a down parka.

As long as I've lived in this apartment, I've screened out danger, slightly distorted by my peephole's convex lens. I've sent danger packing; I've shooed him down the stairs. But things were changing. I couldn't stay in the apartment much longer. I couldn't stay there forever. It smelled like David.

In the afternoon, I cleaned out the medicine cabinet. I dumped David's deodorants, all travel sized, in the wastebasket. I poured his colognes down the sink. He never wore them; he just collected them. Stocking stuffers from a decade of Christmases.

I stuffed the laundry into the washer, unsorted. My red blouse bled all over David's jockey shorts and tee shirts, tinting them pink. She warned me this would happen. Why don't I ever listen? I crammed David's underwear into the steel maw of the garbage chute. They stuck in its throat just above the ground floor. I imagined weeks of garbage choking the chute, backing up onto my kitchen floor. Surely, the super would clean things up; he took care of everything.

I flushed Tweety Bird down the toilet. I'd forgotten to feed him. To celebrate Saturday night, I slipped into bed without my nightie, just Tuesday's panties on. Poor David. He didn't know what he was missing.

Sometime after midnight, the ax murderer called again. I wrapped the rumpled sheets around me. The eye shadow. It had to be the eye shadow.

On Sunday, I said a prayer for Tweety Bird. After I got dressed, I considered calling David's mother, but what could I say; "Is David there?" And, if so, what then? "David, I'm a parakeet murderer, a cologne dumper, an underwear dyer, and, by the way, I want you to come home." No. She had warned me never to do that: ladies who call men on the phone do not get called back.

I did not call David.

I did not wear raggedy underwear.

I did not point.

I did not put my eye makeup on too thickly.

I did not chew with my mouth open.

I did not wear my tight skirt.

I stood up straight, my hair pulled back, my ears unpierced. I did not call attention to myself. I wore a not-too-tight skirt, no heart on my sleeve, modest jewelry, low heels. I smiled pleasantly, but not too much, just barely to the gums. I made the best of what I had without making too much of it. I was nice. I was alone. I wondered why. And I heard you over and over—because you do not cook, do not shave your legs, do not dust the furniture often enough, because your telephone is listed, because you cross your legs at the unladylike knees, because you forget to write thank-you notes; you read in light too dim; you laugh too loudly, don't cover your mouth when you yawn, and, yes, I think you bite your nails and drink alone. Men don't make passes at women in glasses—or in bottles. A man weds a chaste girl but never a chased girl. Men date career women; they marry career wives . . .

You and I alone in our white-walled rooms. I forgave you. I hope that you forgave me. I wondered what you, what she, would say if you, if she, were here. It would be something useful, something inappropriate, something heartbreaking. Why don't you come to see me? You never come to see me. Absence makes the heart grow fonder. You never come to see me.

When the ax murderer called again, I let the phone ring. On the fourteenth ring, I thought, maybe it's David. But it was not David.

"I'm sorry," the nurse said. "She passed away this morning. There was nothing we could do. It was quiet. She never did regain consciousness. She didn't say anything. I mean, she couldn't . . ."

"It's okay," I said, "she still talks to me."

"Oh," the nurse said, her voice strange.

Some things, my mother told me, go better unsaid. "I'm sorry," I said.

"So am I," said the nurse.

On Monday, I arrived at work on time. In the ladies' room, I slicked some sparkly eye shadow on my lids. Carol teetered in on her high heels.

"Well, good morning Mary Sunshine," she said. "Nice to see you caught the boat this morning. FYI—there's a message to call David on your desk. Been sitting there since Friday. Everything okay between you two?"

I smiled. I watched her draw lips over her lips, flick a pinkie for pointier definition.

"It's happening." She sighed. She crinkled her nose at herself in the mirror, patted erase over a crow's foot. "Middle-age. I'm becoming my mother. See you in the salt mines—another day, another wrinkle."

I knew what she meant. My arm falls off; my mother's arm sprouts. I part my lips; her voice slips out. I bite my nail; her nail grows back. Her ribs brace me when mine crack. My lungs fill with her.

Worse things could happen.

Summer Girls

⤻   ⤸

I am not a fanciful man. But the first time I saw her, I stood there, my jaw flapping like a poorly set jib.

"Jesus," Cappy said. Cappy's the pilot of the ferry, the *Harbor Siren*. "What's the matter with you? You're paler than a ghost with the summer complaint."

My tongue lolled, lazy and useless, a seal on the rocks. "Not a thing," I managed to say. "I'm just fine."

"Then uncleat her," Cappy said, "and take the fares."

I was sixteen and green as spring, and I'd never seen anyone like her. She was so beautiful she made you grope for words. After all these years, I still don't have it down exactly. Her hair hung dark as a cormorant's wings, shearing off her shoulders when she turned. Her shoulders were bare and tanned a brown nearly as dark as her hair except her hair had a red cast to it like chestnuts before they split their shells. Her white dress puckered up in little tufts. I don't know what the material is called, but it rubbed against her smooth brown skin in nubs that I could feel. But her eyes, her eyes surprised me most, blue and cool beneath all that thick, black hair. Her eyes were queenly, overlooking her cheeks as if their sockets were towers. She must have been ten years older than me. Cappy followed my eyes and said, "'Bet nobody'd kick *her* out of the lower berth." Cappy can be a coarse s.o.b., and that's the God's truth.

I collected fares on the *Siren* that day, first, on the upper deck; then I went forward. It sounds foolish, but I put off going aft to take her fare as long as I could because I thought if I got near her I'd forget to breathe.

130

I didn't. But when she dropped the two quarters—the fare was still fifty cents then—into my palm, the warmth of them from her hand made my bones turn into water. I lost my sea legs for a minute, and I thought I might roll with the boat. Then she withdrew a little white change purse from her dress pocket and unfolded a crisp, green bill into my hand. She smiled and asked, "What's your name?"

My tongue stuck to the roof of my mouth as I answered, "Emerson, ma'am." I wanted to add that everybody on the island called me Emery, but I couldn't.

She tucked the purse away and said, "Thank you, Emerson. That's a little something extra for you."

No more than that, but in her voice the words sounded unlike any I'd heard before. On that day I got my first tip. And on that day I fell in love for the first time. It never even occurred to me to ask her name.

Her given name was Melissa Hall, but her parents called her Lissa. The Truxton Halls were summer people from north of Boston. Their history, like everything else on the island, quickly became common knowledge. As my mother liked to say, living on an island is like being a songwriter whose songs everyone sings as if they were already public domain. The Halls' song might have been public domain, but the Halls weren't. Island people didn't mix with summer people back then. But there wasn't an island boy who didn't stroll past the Halls on the South Road around dusk hoping for a glimpse of Melissa Hall down by the tennis courts.

I saw her once. The Halls had just arrived. The lilacs were blooming. She stood by the road, tennis racket in hand, the fading breeze flirting with her skirt. I was going to walk on by like I hadn't seen her, but she called my name softly. "Emerson," she said. "Beautiful evening, isn't it?"

"Yes ma'am," I said. And I couldn't think of anything else to say, so like some imbecile I said, "Going to play tennis?"—when even a rock would know someone holding a tennis racket wasn't about to go bicycling or mackerel fishing.

"Do you play?" she asked me quickly.

"No ma'am," I said, and I could feel blood rise in my face like prickly heat.

"Well," she said, swinging her racket back and forth, "I guess I'll just have to wait for my partner." She smiled, teasing, though I don't think she ever knew the full effect of her beauty, how it left all the island boys rummy and reeling. And I walked on.

The next summer she got her partner for real. The Truxton Halls held the wedding party out on the lawn. They even posted a notice on the *Harbor Siren* inviting the locals to the party. And a few went, although most of us contented ourselves with walking along the road like we weren't even aware of the party, grabbing a gawk on the sly. I did.

Colored umbrellas dotted the lawn. A band played, and some couples danced down by the shore. Long tables of food and drink lined the right-of-way to the water. Ladies in dresses and men in summer suits sprouted like wildflowers against the green—so many people it took me a while to find her. But there she was, maybe only two hundred feet away and all in white. She had kicked off her high heels, and she must have stepped on the hem of her dress, because a loop of lace hung tattered, smudged with mud. But it hardly mattered, because her eyes gleamed blue light and her bare, brown feet danced in the grass. She held some icy drink in her hand. I could hear the cubes clink in the glass, see the glass all foggy and dewed. And I thought: if I were that glass in her hand, I would feel just like that—cold and sweaty.

After supper, I walked back again by the Halls' house. Gas party lights cast shadows on the lawn. Crisscrossing, the lamps, strung like pearls, tangled lights and shadows together like snarls of jewelry. In the dark, the guests flitted beside the gardens. I looked for her, but I could not make her out. In the darkness I saw her two white shoes, empty in the roadside grass. And I guessed she had already gone off on her honeymoon.

I think her husband's name was Douglas, Douglas Light. I can hardly remember anymore. But the next summer when he handed Melissa onto the *Siren*, she was pregnant.

"Look like her husband got to her before you could," Cappy said, and he laughed his ugly shriek of a laugh, scree, scree, scree, like gulls scolding intruders at the dump. Scree, scree, scree. I pretended I hadn't heard a thing.

Melissa Hall—I could never think of her by her new name, Lissa Light—sat on the forward deck with her husband. I remember the sun full on her face, her black hair, pinned back by the wind and bright with pearls of sea spray. She sat as wooden as a figurehead. She did not talk to the man, her husband, by her side. And she kept her hands folded flat, one on the other, on the swell of her stomach. Watching her, I wished I could place my hand beside hers, where I fancied her husband placed his, to feel the first kicks. But I would never dare. I barely dared think about it.

In my dreams, she came to me with gardenias pinned in her hair, and, even in my dreams, I did not touch her. I breathed her like dark air at night, like the smell of summer grass, but I did not touch her brown, brown skin or the white puckers of her cotton dress. It was enough to watch her from the corner of my dreams.

The next summer, she arrived with a baby girl in her arms but no husband by her side.

"Jesus," Cappy said, "I wish my old lady looked that good after birthing our rug rats."

I wanted to tell Cappy to shut his mouth, but I was only the deckhand.

"Wouldn't mind putting in for the night in her port, eh?" And he rasped, scree, scree, scree.

Cappy talked like that partly to bait me. He knew—I guess the whole island knew—I loved her, the way I was always gaping like a hooked fish. I was as loopy as a teenage girl, plucking petals: loves me; loves me not—like some unstrung fool. But somehow, whenever I saw her, I was sixteen years old again and seeing her for the first time.

She brought the summer with her, packing it into her steamer trunk like a bathing suit. Always the same summer, the first summer, the only summer. She hit me like sunstroke, made me light blind and dizzy—an easy target for Cappy's jibes. I knew it. But I hated Cappy just the same. I pitied his wife, and I loved Melissa all the more.

I did not covet her, understand. At least I do not think I did. I don't think I once thought of myself as her groom, my elbows resting on the oilcloth at the table's head, my boots by the back door, my nighttime hands on her bare shoulders. I loved her like . . . I don't know exactly. I'm not a man natural with words, but I loved her like you might love the roses rambling on a neighbor's fence, a lilac leaning, bending under its own grapey weight, over a No Trespassing sign. The ones you cannot pick.

The baby, Jennifer, favored her mother, dark-lashed blue eyes, black hair. Each summer she inched higher against her mother's leg, rising like spring watermarks. They stood hand-in-hand on the forward deck coming and going. But the husband never came again.

Then the talk started. First few summers, the story ran, the husband stayed behind to build up the business. Then another woman entered the story, whispers about divorce. Back then, no one got divorced. But Lissa Light became Melissa Hall again, and the talk got mean—that Melissa Hall was drinking and running around, dragging herself lower than Cappy's wife. The gossip grew fangs.

Summer to summer, I would have none of it, because I knew the grapevine, how it twists around everything, how it roots in the dirt. I went about my business day to day, working as deckhand on the *Siren*. I married Minister Black's daughter, Donna, just like people had been saying I would for years, and we started our family, Justin, first, then Mildred, named after Donna's mother. And all this time I loved Melissa Hall, and sometimes at sunset I still strolled up the hill on the South Road past the Halls' place.

I married Donna the year electricity came to the island, run over in an underwater cable. Halls were one of the first to have electricity. All lit up, the place looked almost as nice as the night Melissa got married.

Donna and I were married in the island Congregational Church, and we had our reception at the Grange Hall where baskets of tomatoes, waiting to be judged in the Harvest Days Fair, had to be shoved against the wall so they didn't get danced on. We honeymooned on the island in my mother's shore cottage. And that was that.

Donna made a good island wife. She was no beauty like Melissa Hall, but she could bake blueberry pie so the crust browned up right, and she cleaned mackerel neat, spine-slit, where some wives wouldn't. Unlike Cappy's wife, she was hardworking. She didn't drink, then sleep off half the day. She read stories to the kids. And she forgave me my foolishness for the Hall girl, because she knew, I suppose, that that love would never be brought to bear on our life.

From the time she was about twenty-six, I watched the Hall girl growing old before me. And I stayed loyal to her through time. Her beauty did not wear out, did not wilt like some women's will; it just deepened on her. Her laughs creased into her skin. Her eyes burned blue and smart. In her early forties, she wore her beauty almost like courage. She was fierce.

When I was thirty-five, so Melissa Hall must have been forty-five or so, Mrs. Truxton Hall passed away, and Mr. Truxton Hall passed the island house along to Melissa and Jennifer. He retired to their home near Boston. I never saw him again.

There were no longer parties on the lawn. Melissa Hall no longer played on the tennis courts, which grew over with grass, and the girl, Jennifer, played graveyard tag there at dusk with the island kids. The gardens choked with weeds, and the perennials, the bleeding heart and primroses, ran riot, spreading beyond their proper beds. I rarely saw Melissa except on the *Siren,* but I knew she was home by the yellow squares of electric light in the semidark crouch of the house on the hill.

One day, as the ferry listed, everything shifted. As I took Melissa Hall's fare—a dollar-fifty by then—she asked me, "Emerson, how many years have I been crossing the ferry like this with you?"

"About twenty-odd years now, I guess."

"Twenty years," she said. "And in all that time you've never once called me by my name."

"Yes ma'am," I said.

"Please call me Lissa," she said. "Everyone does."

And I did. But her name felt odd, bothersome, like a jaw-breaker you roll in your mouth.

Then she said, "And please drop by the house sometime for some coffee and a chat," as if it would be the most natural thing in the world. "I'm lonesome here," she added, then turned to her daughter Jennifer, leaving me cold and sweaty in the wake of the words.

When Cappy heard of it, he said, "You're home, man. You're the next in line. You're in like Flynn and halfway under the sheets already." He made me sick. Scree, scree, scree. "I'd let that black widder spin her stickum around me any day and eat me whole." Scree, scree, scree.

Sometimes the ferry shrank around us like a leaky inner tube, squeezing Cappy and me so close together I felt like diving overboard. A boat's a tight place, like an island. As I pulled up on forty, I found myself deep in these wishing spells where I longed to be shut of my life, my job, God help me, my family and my wife, and, yessir, even myself. I had always been a level-headed man, content with my way, practical, like most island men. But I looked at Cappy, and I listened to Cappy, and I felt trapped, like I'd been looking at him and listening to him for two hundred years. Somewhere people ate foods I never tasted, sang songs I never heard, beat the moonlight into the thin gold of morning sun with their feet. She put words into my head. She sang strange songs to me while I slept. My dreams danced to secret music.

One night I followed my legs up the hill, up the rotting stair treads to the house on the hill, and I knocked on Melissa Hall's door. I don't know what pushed me there. It wasn't courage, exactly, and it wasn't lust. But I found my way there as surely as sugar ants find the bowl on the kitchen table. When Melissa Hall answered the door, she wasn't surprised to see me.

Those shortening days near the season's end were the happiest of my life. Melissa and I would sit on the porch and drink lemonade or coffee, depending on the weather. We talked about almost nothing—the prices at the island store, the rain that was surely coming or not coming, errands we had to run to the mainland. But I treasured the words like they were the gnarliest riddles. At night, the words resounded in my head like the clang of the bell buoy off the point, keeping me awake with the pleasure of it. I puttered around the Hall place, almost like a husband might, weeding dandelions from the garden beds, thinning the perennials, fixing Jennifer's swing although she was grown, replacing the stair treads, mending the screens in the master bedroom, caulking the window panes. How Donna kept her silence, I don't know, because the grapevine tangled up with talk of Melissa Hall and me. But nothing untoward ever happened between us. I just wanted to be near her, near as the next rocker on the porch.

Maybe Donna sensed that. She was a forgiving woman, putting up with loose treads on her own back stairs while I hammered fresh boards in place for Melissa Hall. When our garden at home sprouted with weeds, Donna went out and took over the weeding. She never said a reproachful word. For a short time, I felt like a man who had split time in half and himself in two and lived in two different worlds at once. Those shortening days near the season's end were the saddest of my life.

I took that winter hard, its purple shadows stretching thin as knife blades on the snow. The Halls' house, with snow sifting over the windowsills and banked up on the porch, looked heartless, icy—its windows blank, its doors boarded up. When the harbor iced up, as it sometimes will for a few days, I thought I would go mad. I tried talking to Donna about the same things I might have talked to Melissa Hall about, but the words dropped between us, weighted down with their ordinariness. Something was missing. I thought of the Halls' lawn in summer, yellow with dandelions, bright as promises. Beautiful weeds. The winter wore on and on.

The day Melissa Hall came back, I carried her trunk aboard, and I actually handed her down onto the *Siren*, touching the hand that had opened a white change purse, swung a tennis racket, worn Douglas Light's ring, folded over the mound of her stomach. I helped Jennifer aboard, too, and, if Melissa had said the word, I'd have carried them up to their house on my shoulders. But she didn't. When we got across, I helped them off. Cappy winked at me, but I willed myself blind to his leering, old face, because I was determined that it was going to be a perfect day.

That night I bolted supper. I was eager to be off up the hill, take my place on the porch, tell her how much I had missed her, or only talk of this and that. But when I crested the hill, the windows in the house were dark, except on the western side, where a sun set in each one. I knocked, but nobody answered. I thought I heard Jennifer's voice rising off the water, down by the pier where the teenagers drank beer, too remote to hear my knocking. I knocked again. I noticed the dooryard lilac was browning out although it was early June yet, the purple curling back into brown. Then I heard something from above, Melissa's low voice murmuring through the bedroom window, through the screens I'd patched last summer. I heard this sound like an unoiled saw cut into the green wood of me— *scree, scree, scree.*

When I was a boy, an old man, older than I am now, used to tell stories about shipping out, winters wasting on the sea, so lonely that the sailors heard the mermaids sing. Only, when you followed the voice to the singer, close enough to press your mouth onto the song and make the chorus yours, you found yourself snuggling up to a blubbery-carcassed walrus who rolled off your closeness with a splash. A single splash.

People say the daughter, who's in her thirties now, is the image of her mother. I couldn't say. It's like I was blinded to Melissa. She came and went on the ferry; I took her fare. But she was just another passenger. One summer, she didn't come at all. The grapevine had it she'd married somebody in Boston, and they go summer somewhere else, on the Cape. She sold the house, although Jennifer still comes back sometimes with her husband and daughter. They stay at the Old Lighthouse Inn.

Everything changes, even here on the island. A practical man would say that you can't lose something you never had in the first place. But none of it matters. They don't matter to me anymore. Melissa and Jennifer, they're just summer girls; they come and go.

Donna died last winter, and I took it pretty hard. It was like having truth fall on you all at once, like hearing a voice through a bedroom window and knowing in an instant: it could have been anyone; it could have been me.

The days fall from me like dry petals. And the years keep doing what they do best. They come and go like summer girls, pinning bruised gardenias in their hair.

About the Author

Joan Connor is the author of *Here on Old Route 7: Stories* (University of Missouri Press). She is Assistant Professor of Creative Writing at Ohio University in Athens.